Sick & Twisted

A collection of dark fairytales

CW01483616

What do a cunning princess, a mad maiden, mischievous pigs, a dangerous secret, an evil king, and a lovesick mermaid have in common?

They are all the twisted versions of fairy tales you thought you knew as a child. Those tales that used to make a regular appearance in all your dreams and fantasies.

But dreams can turn on you, creating a string of nightmares you will never escape.

Vengeance of Aerwyna
Based loosely on
The Mermaid of Gob Ny Ooyl Manx Fairy Tales
Lianne Willowmoon

Dedication
I dedicate this story to my daughter Aireal. She loves mermaids and Halloween/horror as much as I do. And this is a mix of both. I love you my little dreamer!

Edwan thought when his wife died, he would never love again. That was until the beautiful Aerwyna shows up on his boat. However, when love turns to vengeance, no one is safe… not even her love.

*Not all stories have
happy endings…*

Edwan stood at the window in his small, unkempt cabin. Since his wife had passed away just two months before winter had set in, he had given up trying to keep up with the tedious everyday things such as picking up after himself. It was just him, and since she was gone, would always be just him. He vowed to never love another.

He moved to pull his heavy, flannel rain jacket over his long muscular arms. The blanket of snow was melting and that, for him, meant that it was time to start his fishing business back into full swing. The past couple of years, he hadn't had the best of luck with catching the bigger game. His wife's funeral cost him more than he could afford, but he didn't complain. The winter had been a long one after that, for he had to make do with two meals a day; the last two weeks he made do with one each day to stretch what little supplies he was able to

5

afford himself. He had spent the entire winter either crying over his loss and loneliness… or praying for a better season on the sea to catch up and to survive from.

He worked his way out to The Valentine. His vessel was all he had when he met his wife. She chose to rename her when they married. She had told him that The Loner wasn't a loner anymore and he had chuckled, allowing her to gift his vessel with the name The Valentine. He smiled and nodded at the cherished memory as he climbed the boarding plank to her deck. He made sure to double check everything; the winters were hard around this area; he needed to make sure she was sea ready for the weekend ahead. Luckily, after a thorough examination, there were no repairs needed this year. That was both a blessing and a relief.

Friday morning, he packed what little food he had left for travel in a box and filled six large waterskins with fresh well water. He boarded The Valentine and prepared to set sail for the weekend. The sea was a bit rough at first, but the further he sailed away from the mainland toward the Canaan Isle where he always did his fishing, the sea seemed to calm for him. He had been going there since he was 15 with his father, just over 14 years ago. He arrived within a mere three hours and set his boat, anchoring it near the shore. He would start his fishing at night and hope for bigger game that had been growing through the winter months.

That evening, he awoke and set his nets. First throw, he prayed for a better haul that he had been pulling from the harsh sea. As he reeling in the net, he caught a few dozen smaller fish, that he placed into the well. He sighed. It had to get better. He cast his nets a second time, praying again for good luck. Reeling it in, he started to lose hope that this was going to net him anymore than smaller fish which didn't bring in much at all at the local market.

He couldn't afford to have another bad year. It might end with him selling his boat and moving on if he did. He had already sought out several buyers for The Valentine if things went horribly. He said prayers that it wouldn't come to that though. The thought of selling her made him sob like a child; it was like losing the last part of his wife.

The third time he cast the net, he prayed again. "Allod, thrice is my lucky number! Please, see fit to grace me with your blessings from your mighty home!"

He felt a huge, strong tug on the net and the bow of the ship bounced upon the wave in response. He watched wide eyed as the net reel pulled as if something were struggling to get free. His heart leapt as he started to wind the rope, pulling the net to the surface with the net crane. As it pulled over onto the planks, he eagerly unwound the net… and stood with his eyes wide, his mouth gaping at the creature that lay before him.

Staring back at him were the most beautiful green eyes he had ever witnessed. Long flowing auburn hair flowed around shoulders of paled, blushed skin. Features soft, and heavenly, lay upon the face of his catch. Small and fragile physique, breasts bare to the beauty of nature and a waist that barely graced an 8 in size lay before him. However, in all her beauty, it was what lay beneath that waist that intrigued his curiosity.

The moonlight shone down on glistening scales; the hues of blue, green and red vibrant with the glittering light from the heavens shining down upon them. Her hips fused together in a beautiful hourglass shape and led to fins much like a dolphin's. He gasped as he stepped back, for a moment stunned at what lay before him trapped within the confines of The Valentine's nets. He placed a gloved hand to his mouth and closed it, blinking.

"My Allod, are you… what I think you are, my beautiful creature?"

She looked at him, a bit of fear in her eyes, as she stuttered her response. "Please, do not harm me and I shall give you anything you wish. You have nothing to fear from me, simple fisherman."

He cleared his gruff throat and nodded, reaching to start unwrapping her. "I do not wish to harm you, my lady. I am amazed and mesmerized by you, to be quite honest."

She helped him how she could and as soon as his nets were free, she flipped herself to the side of the boat, disappearing into the sea below. He stood, disappointed he didn't get to have a longer conversation with her before she left his presence. Just when he thought he would never see her again, he turned to see her posing herself on a large, smooth wet stone to the side of the boat. He walked over, removing his gloves and sitting off the side of the bow near her.

"Thank you for your kindness, sir. Most wouldn't have let me go. You proved your heart. What can I give to you in return?"

He chuckled and hung his head. "There isn't much I can ask of such a beauty. I don't make a habit of taking advantage of friends, which I hope that you might become."

She smiled and nodded happily. "I would love that. We don't see many humans out here. You are a first."

"Most have given up this area for the larger areas. My boat can't handle the larger area's waters, so I am forced here. However, this evening, I wouldn't say that is a curse. Meeting you has been a pleasure beyond anything I could have hoped."

She smiled softly, "Men usually see us as meal tickets. You seem to notice me much more. For that I am appreciative. May I ask your name?"

He took a deep breath, still awed by her. "My name is Edwan, my lady."

They sat and talked for the rest of the night. They talked about life under the sea, and what it was like riding dolphins into the sunset. She asked him about his wife, and he was glad to be able to tell her their story. The moonlight slowly faded with the morning sun. As he saw it, he began to yawn, realizing that the entire evening of fishing had gone with the settling of the moon.

"Do you happen to have an apple, dear Edwan?"

He stopped and laughed. "What an odd request,

but as it happens to be, I do."

She giggled. He had to smile at the request, going in and digging out one of his preserved green apples from his food box. He reappeared on deck with it and her eyes lit up. Reaching forward, he held the apple in his hand. She gracefully reached out, taking his hand in hers and exchanging the apple for a small green jewel.

"It is called a mermaid tear. They are rare. It is my gift to you, as is what you will receive the rest of the weekend. It is my thank you for the apple."

And with that, she flipped into the sea, swimming into the depths. He took the jewel and placed it for safekeeping in the lock box near his bed. He laid, his curiosity about the beautiful woman keeping him awake. Eventually, he did drift away to sleep. He slept the day away in peace.

*****

That evening, he made his way to the nets. Casting it the first time, he saw the crane struggle to keep up with the pulling and tugging below. Stunned, he reeled in the nets to find not only six dozen smaller fish, but about four dozen larger ones and three giant fish as well! Excited, he cast it a second time, bringing up just as much as the first cast. After the third, his well was full. He plugged it and locked it down, ready to head home. Before setting sail, he went ashore and left another apple on the stone.

"Thank you, my friend with no name. I am blessed today because of you."

As he boarded and looked back, the apple was gone. He smiled, content on the events of the weekend. Getting back to shore, he started to barter off his catch and was pleased to find that he had made more that weekend than he did half the season the previous year. He hoped and prayed for one more good run, before things settled at least. He, however, admitted it was only because of his new friend, that he had done that well. For that, he was thankful.

*****

The next weekend, he prepped his boat and set sail for the isle. The sea was much calmer than it had been the weekend before. He set up his nets and cast four times, not bringing in much but more than he normally would. Looking to the rock, he smiled and thought for a moment. Maybe...

Grabbing two apples, he went and set on the rock. He sliced one and began to eat his snack when a familiar voice appeared. "That one for me, dear Edwan?"

He smiled as the mermaid came up on the rock beside him. No longer fearing him, she reached over and snatched the apple, coveting it before slowly munch on it. He laughed.

"You didn't think that I came out here just for the fish, did you? I have yet to learn a name for you, though."

She glanced to him and a puzzled gaze appeared on her face. "I do not have a name. Mermaids often do not name their young. I have a wonderful idea!

Why don't you choose a name for me?"

He stopped and thought hard for a moment. Looking at her brilliant green eyes smiling at him, anxiously awaiting a name to be spoken from his lips, he remembered the name that his wife had given him if they had ever had a daughter. "Aerwyna. The name holds a special place in my heart, and I shall never forget it. So that shall be your name."

She smiled, and a glint of tears appeared in her eyes. "Aerwyna. I love it, dear Edwan. Thank you."

They sat and ate their apples as the moon rose to full shine. Aerwyna then bid him good night and told him she would see him the next weekend. As with the weekend before, she blessed his well with more than he could carry. He smiled when he thought of Aerwyna. His wife would have loved to see her.

*****

Below the sea's surface, Aerwyna sat in her cave and thought about Edwan, the man from the land. She was taken with his soft glowing blue eyes and the way he regarded her. The more her thoughts possessed him, the more her heart did as well. She had heard of the term love but had never experienced it. Perhaps, Edwan felt the same. Although she was shy and reserved, she knew she should ask him how he felt and see if he shared her affections. Perhaps she would the next time she saw him. Perhaps he would eventually stay with her. Only time would tell.

*****

Edwan went through the week making minor repairs to his home from the winter. He cleaned up some and was feeling a bit better about life since he met Aerwyna. He had a new outlook on life and couldn't wait to go back out the following weekend. He had made sure, when he was selling off his last catch, that he picked up some extra apples. This time, he choose shiny red delicious apples instead of his usual green ones. Something sweet for his special friend. He had also purchased a small open tiered gem locket on a chain, in which he placed the mermaid's tear gem safely. He hung it around his neck, and placed it inside his shirt, so questions wouldn't be asked. He didn't want to give away his secret.

He loaded up his boat and prepared to head out, making sure to place four apples inside his food box. There looked to be a storm brewing. He hoped that it would starve off for the weekend and not ruin his weekly plans.

The sea was rough and harsh. Once he anchored, he stayed inside and watched the swells to make sure he was in no danger. He then found himself praying that Aerwyna was in no danger as well. The storm lasted through the first night and into the morn, where he had fallen asleep for the day. That afternoon, he awoke with a jolt at a knocking on the side of his boat. Scrambling to get outside, he saw Aerwyna in the water with a relieved smile.

"Oh, my dear Edwan, I am glad that you made it through the storms! I was concerned!

He nodded to the sky and laughed. "No storm can keep me down, my sweet Aerwyna! I am a fisherman… storms are nothing to me. Besides, you didn't think that it would stop me from our weekend snack, did you?"

She bit her lip and nodded, swimming over to the wet rock and climbing up. He left the safety of his boat and brought the apples, sitting with her through the day. He knew that he would be exhausted, but it would be worth it.

*****

On the last night before winter set in, Edwan anchored the Valentine and had brought a special treat. He thought that she might want to try some caramel on her apple. It was a tradition in his family that near the end of the fall, that they would sit by the fire and enjoy fresh melted caramel, apples and cider. It was thrilling to get to introduce her to this!

He waited, setting up a small fire on the rock. The autumn weather had set in and he brought a heavy blanket to sit on the rock with. Just as he had guessed, she climbed the rock and smiled at him.

"What is this, dear Edwan? It smells divine!"

"It is called caramel. It is sweet and tastes wonderful on apple slices. I thought we might celebrate a wonderful time these last few months. I know that I may not be able to make it out here during the winter months and thought that if this was the last time for a while, we would see one another, that we might want to do something special."

She glanced to him, a sad expression catching the corners of her eyes and lips dragging them downward. "I guess that I had not thought of that, my dear Edwan. It will be difficult for you sailing here in the frozen time. I am saddened, but I do understand. Promise me that as soon as you can in the flowering time, that you will return to me once again!"

"There is nothing that can hold me back from it, my sweet Aerwyna!"

She smiled and wrapped her arms around him, hugging him deeply. "I have something to show you! I can only use this once, so I choose you!"

She backed up and took a deep breath, grabbing her mermaid tear. As she did so, he watched in absolute amazement as her fin stretched and shifted, shortening and flexing. Her scales started to spilt, blood dripping off them onto the rock. He jumped up and watched the horror as the tail split into two forms. A glowing red energy appearing around them both as she screamed in agony. There was a blinding red light that made him turn his face from her for a moment as her screaming faded. He feared turning and seeing what she had done to herself. At the sound of her gentle voice, she called his name.

"Turn to me, dear Edwan. And see what I am offering to you."

"I do not wish to see the horrors of what you have done to yourself!"

She laughed. "There is no horror here for me. This is something every mermaid goes through in time."

He slowly spun and opened his eyes, shocked at what he saw before him. Blood and scales spanned the rock. She was in the water, with a shell, slowly washing it away. Once the rock was clean, she climbed up once more and stood... she STOOD! Her fin had split into two perfectly formed fins, resembling legs. Although there were a few bleeding spots still, the scales we growing fast over them, covering her legs. Edwan stared in shock as she smiled. He admired her body for a moment as she begged for his approval.

"Please, say something! Anything!"

"You are the most beautiful creature. And by far the most unique one I have ever encountered as well!" He couldn't help but stare at her almost human form. He legs, now completely covered in scales shone like gems in the moon and firelight mixture, giving them a fire and ice type look. Her thighs were still the same hourglass shape, only now she had all the more inviting parts of a woman. His eyes were immediately drawn to the space between them, where there was smooth skin instead of scales. "You have human female parts?"

She smiled. "Once we go through the transformation, yes. I am as much human as any other woman you have seen. Please, come…"

He walked forward as she took his hand, taking it slowly to the warmth of her pudenda. He took no time at all caressing her, as she groaned underneath the pressure. Feeling her swell beneath his touch made him want to ravish her in every way he could before morning. As if hearing his most private of thoughts and desires, she opened her legs a bit wider and pressed his fingers gently past the threshold of her lips to the moist places inside. He pulled her to him with his other hand and took his lips to hers in a hard and wanton kiss, full of not passion, but the need to be inside her. The drive to make her scream loud enough that the mainland heard her pleasure. As he kissed her, he continued his probing as he slid a finger up as far as he could get it inside her and felt the inside of her get hot and wet at his invasion of her privacy. She groaned and ground her newly formed sex against his hand, wanting to feel more.

"I want to make you scream my name, Aerwyna!"

"My heart already does, my voice yearns to follow suite, my dear Edwan."

He swooped her up and laid her across the blanket, the cold Autumn air not a concern now as he was overheated with lust and ripped off his shirt. She watched as he took his clothes off, having never seen a male form, and took a deep breath as he unbuttoned his pants. His hard on springing to life from the confines of his cotton skivvies. She couldn't resist the urge to reach up and take it into her hands, enjoying the feel of him between her fingers. He groaned as she played and caressed him, lovingly at first and the harder as she noticed him groaning more and more.

"Take me into your mouth, sweet Aerwyna!"

She looked up at him and them to her hands, slowly licking the tip of his hard on. He groaned, and threw his head back, and she delighted in seeing him happy. Wanting to hear the low guttural groan again, she took him into her mouth and ran her tongue down the shaft hard. He groaned louder and grabbed her head, forcing him into her mouth over and over. Releasing himself, he felt his stress dissolve as his seed hit her throat. Looking down at her shining green eyes, she laid back on the blanket, legs spread, inviting him to indulge himself in her. He peered down on her, stopping to admire the changes he saw to her form. The scales on the inside of her thighs were sold and smooth, not even looking as if they were separate scales at all. Her folds were a bluish tint as the rest of her skin was, and there were touches of pink on the undersides of her delicately laid labia. He moved down into position between her legs and without giving her a chance to steady herself took his mouth to her, licking up from the bottom to the top, spreading her folds with his tongue. She gasped, pulling his head to her and holding him there.

"You tasted sweet, my dear Edwan. I hope that I taste just as sweet to your mouth."

He lifted only to growl and moan. "Better

than sweet apples, my sweet Aerwyna! The juices that flow from you are a gift from the heavens!"

She laid back and arched her back, grinding herself against his mouth and yearning to feel his tongue probe her. As if answering her request, he stuck his unusually long tongue into her folds and beyond, making her grab his hair and scream in intense pleasure.

"Do not stop, for I fear that I will not be able to handle it! Please, break this seal of chasteness I hold and claim me as yours!"

He reached a hand up and took two fingers to her, shoving them in and out of her quick and hard till she screamed again, her juices flowing out naturally from her. He took his tongue back to his fingers and her folds, cleaning up most of it before he could no longer bear it. He moved quickly and took position, driving his hard on deep within her folds.

He expected pain on the first go, but no... this woman never even flinched as she ground herself against him. Her soft and wet folds gently caressing him as he pulled out and shoved back into her. He pinned her hands above her head as he took the other down to caress the scales of her thighs. Her veins beneath the scales pulsated, making them move as if she had snakes underneath them. He watched in both horror and amazement as tentacles came from within her womb to caress his hard on as he violated her. They wrapped around him, the hundreds of tiny suction cups sucking along it as he continued to take her. Feeling his release, he threw his head back and felt himself fill her with his seed. She screamed as the tentacles pulled him into the hilt, pulling the head into her womb and holding it there as she felt her release take hold. He grunted and felt the tentacles massaging him to release again, mesmerized at the feel…

Collapsing at her side, the tentacles still reaching over her leg to massage his hard on back to full go, she climbed on top of him and smiled as she shoved herself on to him, taking him deep within her.

"Let them do their job. You lay still and enjoy this."

Within a few seconds, he felt her insides change as the tentacles pulled him into her womb and began to caress him, making his hard on stronger and harder than before. He closed his eyes and concentrated on the feeling of them working on him, sucking and licking at his form. However, it was a shock when one of them entered the tip and began working on him from the inside out.

He glanced to her frantic. "Shhhhh, trust me. Let them to what they do."

They probed him till he released three more times, exhausting him. He remembered looking at her and smiling as he drifted off to sleep.

He woke the next morning, with his clothes on and in the bed of his boat, with a note by his bed that simply read "till spring".

This continued for many years. As Edwan grew older so did Aerwyna. But this is where our tale takes a turn for the worse...

*****

Edwan had grown older to the point that he couldn't make the trip out any longer. Although Aerwyna had aged gracefully, as mermaids lived a sight longer than a human, he had become broken down too much to make the haul. He hired two young boys to start fishing for him. He even bought a second boat to help things along, providing for all three of them and their families as well.

Gerald, a strapping 20-year-old, had a wife and new son at home. Marvel, who was barely 18, had just gotten married and was hoping to start a family soon. Edwan realized this would be a great opportunity for them all. The boys promised to take care of him till he went to be with his wife as well.

The Valentine he passed to Gerald, and the Crescent Moon he put in Marvel's hands. That spring and summer, and even into the fall, was the worst season he had ever had for fish. They hadn't brought back a single haul that measured even a 1/20th of what he had brought in. Puzzled, he thought about it hard. That night, he sighed as he figured it out.

The next morning, the boys had come in to turn in the boat keys for the winter. He begged them to go out one more weekend, thinking he had the solution to the issue. They sighed and told him they would on the off chance it helped them make enough to at least survive the winter months. He told them about the wet stone and the apples. They had laughed at him when he told them story of his beautiful fish friend. They called him names and said that he was crazy. However, to appease the old man, they did as he asked.

That weekend, they prepared the boats for one final run. Loading everything onto the boats and making sure they had a bag of apples, they headed out to the Isle. Finding the stone, they sat the apples out and waited. Before long, Aerwyna appeared. Both of the boys stared in amazement as she climbed the rock and snatched up one of the apples.

"Who might you be and where is my Edwan?"

Gerald stuttered and shook his head in disbelief. "He is older now and not able to make the trip. He hired us to run his boats. He sent these apples to you."

She nodded and smiled warmly at first. "He is aging quickly. It is not fair to humans to age and pass so quickly. Thank you for the apples, young ones."

As she started to leave, he called out once more. "WAIT! He said that you might bless us with fish for the winter? We have families you see, and we are now caring for him as well."

She turned, her green eyes fading. "He did, did he? Well, I guess that I can grant him that request. Cast your nets tonight, and you will be blessed."

As she left, the boys were shocked and excited. They prepared themselves for the evening and slept through the day. That evening, in the hours of the moon, they cast the nets. In 4 casts, both wells were full, and they headed home. When they arrived at the docks, people were overwhelmed by the fish they had brought in. Everyone came and paid them for fish for the winter months. Keeping some for themselves and Edwan, they were anxious to arrive at his home to deliver the good news. Edwan was pleased to know that his offerings of apples still were loved by the mermaid he had a special place for in his heart.

This continued through the next season, adding a third boat to the mix. By the end of the that season, he had grown so wealthy, he bought two more boats. With a total of five now, he would have much more than he needed and wouldn't want for anything. But all good things come to an end...

*****

The first sail of the next season, he sent all five boats out into the isle. He sat back and was waiting to hear from them on Monday morning. However, his weekend was caught short. The boats returned on Sunday, completely empty of any fish.

"I am sorry, Edwan. We went to the spot we always do and set up the ships. Aerwyna came and greeted us. She was rather frantic about there being five boats instead of three. She took the apples, thanked us and waved her hand over the ocean before she disappeared. We caught nothing all weekend."

Edwan thought for a moment and nodded. "Must have been a fluke. We will try again next weekend."

As they left, he sat and pondered why they had come home empty handed. He had given her what she asked, and she had always returned the kindness by providing full wells. He had sent plenty of apples, or so he had thought… maybe he would send more. The next weekend, he made sure to load them up with apples. In many varieties as well. Maybe that would make her happy enough to grant their requests.

Friday night, the winds grew strong and the rain came in heavily. The storm that was brewing was a hard one, taking a few shingles off Edwan's roof in the worst part of it. He sat in his chair and prayed that his men, and Aerwyna were safe. He paced the floor as the storm came to a calm and was thankful it was over. However, he still worried about them.

Monday morning came and went and as he stood by the docks, he was frazzled. His men hadn't returned yet. He paced the wooden planks, desperate for answers. Eventually, he walked home and sat in his home, frantically thinking about the storm. Could they have gotten caught in it? And if so, where were they? Were they hurt? Were they dead?

Aerwyna wouldn't have let them die. She would have helped them for she knew they were important to his survival. In the end, he reasoned that they were catching good loads and they were simply late coming home. He eventually turned in and laid his weary head down to rest. He awoke every hour that night and tossed and turned what little he did sleep.

Something was bothering him to the point of exhaustion. He kept having vivid nightmares of going to the island and finding them dead, laying in the water with his poor Aerwyna in the middle. It was enough to scare him out of sleeping altogether.

The next morning, he headed to the docks. By noon, it was apparent that his men were not returning. Something was very wrong. He went to the closest ship and paid the man to take him out to the isle to find his men. The man was a bit hesitant, not buying his story of the mermaid and the apples, but he took the money and agreed to it because he was desperate for the income. The entire way to the isle, Edwan paced. He hadn't been this concerned since his wife had passed. He leaned over the edge and saw the isle ahead. Raising his eyes in fear, he saw the boats all washed ashore. The storm but have banked them!

For a brief moment, the fear left as he just knew they were alive. "Kind Sir! Those are my boats! If they have banked themselves due to the storm, there is a possibility that my men are safe and alive still. I will pay you double to get us out of here so that I might have someone return to get the ships."

The man, who called himself Dywel, nodded and sighed. "Must be a relief to see that the boats aren't destroyed!"

Edwan yelled back, "Yes, it is! That is my livelihood. I wouldn't eat without them!"

Dywel nodded. "I think I can agree with you there! Same goes for me and mine. How close do you need to be to row ashore, so I can anchor?"

"Here will be fine! I will see how bad the ships are ashore and get my men together. We will be back in a short bit."

He took the row boat on the back of the chartered fishing rig and rowed to the isle. As he got closer, the horrible truth because increasing clear. There were blood marks all over the outside of the boats and all over the rocks along the bank. He began calling for them, asking if anyone could hear him. Once at the bank, he jumped out of the boat and hit the ground running toward the first boat. As he got to the deck, he screamed in terror.

The gentleman who manned this ship was laying on the deck. His arms and legs had been torn off. His chest cavity had been torn open and his entrails were stretched along the wooden planks. His organs, dripping with the cold rain that was coming down now, all hanging out to dry on fishing hooks across the bow of the ship. Most disturbingly, though, was noticing that the heart and eyes had been torn out and were missing. He covered his mouth as he glanced to the other ships, their crewmen were all laid out the same way.

Screaming again, he looked to the shore to see Aerwyna looking at him, standing on her human form legs. She was covered in blood and screamed a shrill that made his eardrums collapse. He covered them, and screamed, the sound coming silently. He moved his hand and panicked as he saw blood dripping from his palms. He heaved a breath and climbed down from the boat screaming at her.

When she talked to him, he could barely

hear her as the last bit of his eardrums were slowly disconnecting and silencing the world. "You took me as your own! I gave you everything you have, only to be abused! By sending more and more men to use me for my power to call the ocean to your needs! These men didn't love me, nor did they respect me! They were using me! They told me that you weren't able to make the ride here, and yet here you are! You look healthy to me!"

As she told him how she felt, he cried and hit his knees. "I am sorry, my sweet Aerwyna! It was not meant! These men had family to feed as well! I was trying to help them as much as take care of myself!"

"YOU USED ME!"

"Not my intentions, I swear to you! Why did you kill them? WHY!?"

"Because I couldn't take my vengeance on you without you being here. And I knew that if I kept them, you would come to me. Don't worry Edwan, you will be joining them soon!"

Before he could react, she shoved him to the ground and straddled him. Taking the large shard of conch shell, she stabbed his right eye and twisted; a blood curdling scream filled the air as the crunching of his eye socket rattled inside his head. She reached down and pulled it free slowly, smiling devilishly at him as she leaned down and put in in her mouth. She made careful work of her twisted form of torment as she kept his nerve endings attached; he felt the pain of her chewing his eyeball and the agony shot through his entire body causing him to go into convulsions. With his good eye, he watched as the blood ran from her mouth and down her chin, dripping down his cheek.

She let him keep his left eye as she tied his convulsing arms above the elbows and legs below the knees with rope. Using the shell, she sawed off his jerking extremities and took the time to devour a few bites of the exposed muscle and tissue before she cut open his chest. She broke his ribcage, one rib at a time causing him to jerk harder beneath her. Pulling his organs out carefully, she laid them to the side; she made sure to caress each one as she did. The last thing he remembered was seeing her carefully remove his heart and smile as she dug her teeth into it; the life-sustaining organ was still beating within the confines of her jaws as they camped shut, the life fading from his bloody carcass…

Shards of Deceit
Iris Sweetwater

Dedication
This one goes out to Andersen, Perrault, and the Grimm brothers for sparking my imagination and the imagination of my beautiful daughter.

A queen's death, an evil curse, and a king obsessed…

The Evil King has taken hold of the kingdom after the death of his wife, and his love of beauty and lavish parties means no room in his cold heart for the orphaned Prince Snow and even less when the prince grows to be more handsome than even the revered ruler.

With his magic, the king will devise a plan to rid all the kingdom of good and beauty in its purest form so that he and his body will remain supreme. But can one wandering girl with a heart of gold put a stop to it?

Enjoy this gender flip of The Snow Queen and Snow White.

The day was a somber one. The queen was to be buried, and everyone in the kingdom was heartbroken due to her death. Young Prince Snow was pitied, but loved by the throngs. His father was less concerned about his welfare than those among his underlings. It was obvious to all, even during such a sad time, that their king only cared about himself. He was extremely handsome, yet appeared to be coldly heartless.

King Snow stood regally beside the coffin. His dark hair glistened in the sunlight. His muscular, strong body was stiff and unyielding, though the small replica of himself, Prince Snow, clung tightly to his hand. Their blue eyes were an exact match. However, the little prince's glistened with tears while the king's remained dry and unaffected. The crowd believed he was being brave for the sake of his son. They had no way of knowing what was really going through his head, even guessing he loved himself so much.

King Snow's charismatic voice spanned the distance of the beautiful, flower strewn field upon which the coffin was set. He addressed his subjects in a tone that stunned the masses. It seemed a bit hurried and callous, for he was in a hurry. He felt the desperate need to stand before his favorite mirror and gain the reassurance that his wife's death had not changed his physical appearance or his standing as the most handsome in the land. Vanity was his mistress. His wife had been only a servant to him that he constantly forced to praise him.

"Our queen is gone, but you are not to be sad. She is no longer in pain and has served her purpose in this world. I remain here to keep this kingdom safe. Look to me if you are worried. I alone can care for all your needs and desires as long as you remain faithful to me. We will survive without a queen. She was a kind and loving woman, but she was not a true ruler. That was my business, and it always shall be. Go forth, say your farewells, and continue with your duties. The prince and I will be unavailable for several days. We need time alone to grieve our loved one's passing."

Once the short speech was finished, the king turned away and pulled the small prince behind him. He never looked back to see the coffin being lowered into its deep hole or watch as the dirt was shoveled over it.

Prince Snow tugged on his father's hands, fighting to go back to where his mother's body was disappearing. He longed to have her hold him in a warm embrace, kiss his cheek, and be told that he was the brightest light in her life. From this point on, his life would be cold and lonely. The mighty king never held his son or soothed his worries. In fact, the king had declared that at ten years of age the prince should act as a man, not the boy he truly was.

"Take the boy," King Snow demanded of the nursemaid. "I have much to do and cannot be concerned with his tears. See to it that they are ended before I see him again. If he must grieve in this manner, then he must do it in his chambers. I cannot abide a sniveling, soft-hearted child at this moment. I lost a wife, and yet you do not see me crying."

The king hurried to the hidden door in his chamber. Behind it was the room that held all his secrets, including his mirrors. No one was allowed to know of its existence. Not even the queen had ever been inside.

He quickly divested himself of his royal clothing. The bejeweled waistcoat and cape were dropped carelessly on the floor, along with his pants and knee-high boots. He stood before the mirrors in all his naked glory. He marveled at the reflection he saw. The vivid blue eyes raked the perfectly sculpted body that the mirror revealed. From every angle the picture remained the same. No one could measure up to the beauty the king possessed; or so he hoped.

"Mirror awaken! Answer my request. Among those in my kingdom, am I still the best? Tell me nothing has changed now that the queen is lost. Assure me that mourning her hasn't been at great cost."

The mirror replied, "No man surpasses you in looks or demeanor. As for the queen, her passing has not changed a thing. As always, only your praises, I sing."

King Snow's heart almost stopped upon hearing a voice from behind him utter, "What was that?". His face showed rage mixed with fear as he spun to glare at the intruder.

"How did you get in here, boy?" he shouted. "How dare you come where you are not invited!"

"But, Father, the door was ajar. I wanted to apologize for making you ashamed with my tears. I couldn't find you, then I noticed the door. Are you a sorcerer?"

"Yes. I am a mighty sorcerer. I can destroy you with just a few words. You should heed this warning. Never step foot in this room again. Forget you ever saw it. If you dare to mention its existence to anyone you will pay a heavy price. This is none of your business. My privacy is important. If you do not obey me, you may find yourself outcast from this kingdom. You do not wish to spend all your life completely alone, do you?" The king retorted, not caring in the least that he was alienating his own son.

"No, sire. I have lost enough recently. This room, and those mirrors, will never be spoken of by me. Please, Father. You are all I have left. Do not be angry with me. It was just that I was shocked to hear a mirror speak. Will the mirrors be mine one day?"

"NEVER! I told you, this is my room. These mirrors belong only to me. Only I can control them. Leave, before I lose what patience I have left," King Snow commanded.

He was seething as he watched the small boy depart. His sanctuary had been invaded, and it made his paranoia much worse. His worst nightmare was the idea of the boy taking his place as the most handsome in the land. The mirrors, and his image in them, enchanted him. Yet, they also brought out his worst self.

*****

Time had passed far too quickly for the king's comfort. His little boy was no longer a child. Today was his eighteenth year. The boy was now a man, with the same handsome face of his father. When the king looked at him, he became afraid, and a deep hatred began to grow in his already black heart. Jealousy was an evil thing. The youthful, unwrinkled skin of the prince was enough to give the older king nightmares. The dreams didn't bode well for the future.

However, the king was aware that his subjects could not be allowed to see the anger or hatred that was consuming him. He must keep up with appearances, or there would be a revolt. So, a party was about to begin. It was to celebrate the prince's new status as an adult. King Snow would make the best of it. After all, he enjoyed parties where he could be looked upon with envy by those less fortunate.

Dancing and merriment were in full swing. The king was having his third pint of whiskey when he paused to observe his son dancing. The prince was surrounded by the most beautiful, unmarried females of the kingdom. That honor had once been his. He began to feel a bit strange, a little lightheaded. It wasn't from the drinks. He held his liquor well. There was something far worse happening to him. He began to feel old.

King Snow allowed the bad feeling to fall to the back of his mind when a lovely maiden bowed before him. The twinkle in her eyes proclaimed her desire for the king. He swiftly tossed aside his cup and grabbed the silky haired maiden by the hand. First, he took her for a spin on the dance floor, then he took her to his chambers for a rowdier game to prove to himself he was still young and handsome.

Holding the naked maiden in his arms, after his lust had been sated, the king asked her an important question. If she answered incorrectly, she would meet her demise that very night.

"My dear, who enchants you the most in all of my kingdom? Tell me the truth," he ordered.

The maiden was no fool. She knew the king to be a vain man. It wouldn't hurt to stroke his ego. He might reward her for her praise. He had never remarried, and every woman in the kingdom had hopes of becoming the queen.

She answered, "You, my king, are the most enchanting man I've ever met. You have fulfilled my fantasies this night."

She wasn't exactly telling an untruth. The king was the most enchanting man she had ever met, for she had yet to be introduced to Prince Snow.

King Snow didn't see through her deception. He was pleased with her answer. It made him feel strong and powerful once more. He sent her away with a promise to bestow jewels and delicious delicacies upon her. He swore he would call her back to his chambers for more elaborate games.

Alone once more, the king began to feel strange again. He couldn't relieve the worry that entered his mind, and there was nothing to distract him. He considered returning to the festivities that continued in the ballroom, but the idea of seeing the prince being fawned upon upset him too much. His gaze went to the door that led to his mirrors. He could sense them calling to him. He didn't resist the pull of their magic. Instead, he followed his obsessive desire.

He greeted his favorite mirror the same as before. "Mirror awaken! Answer my request. Among those in my kingdom, am I still the best?"

To his horror, the answer was not what he expected. The mirror calmly announced, "Though my king is still handsome, he is no longer the best. Your son, Prince Snow, has stood up to the test. It is he that holds the title now. As we speak, it is at his feet the women of the kingdom bow."

Rage beyond reason consumed the king. This atrocity could not be allowed. The prince must die, along with all the children he had sired by the mistresses he had used over the years. None of the illegitimate children held a candle to Prince Snow in intelligence or looks, but the king still imagined them as threats to his title and ego. His obsession with the enchanted mirrors grew stronger, emptying his wicked heart of the last drop of love he possessed.

King Snow summoned the captain of the guards to his chamber. He ordered, "Find all the offspring I have sired over the decades and destroy them. When you have accomplished that task, you must kill the prince and bring his lifeless body to me."

The captain was shocked and devastated by the command. He stammered, "Yyyour Maaajestyy, why would you want the prince to die?"

"He has threatened my life and will do whatever he feels necessary to take the throne from me," the king lied.

Though the captain did not believe his king, he knew he was destined to obey. It tore a hole in his soul, but he gathered the illegitimate children of King Snow and put them to death. However, when he drew near the prince, the agony in his soul proved to be too much. He could not harm the young man, so he ran from the kingdom, never to be seen again.

When King Snow learned of the betrayal, his rage became impossible to control. He summoned the executioner and demanded that the prince be hung for treason. To his credit, the executioner declared, "I will not murder an innocent man, especially the man who will one day be my king."

Rage overpowered reason, and the king strangled the executioner.

*****

Unable to gain control of his now blood-stained heart, the king wanted retribution for the imagined sins against him. He entered the chamber of mirrors, skipped over his favorite, and went to face one that suited his current need for vengeance.

King Snow's eyes turned to black as he held his hands aloft and chanted the spell, "Shatter and freeze, my wicked friend. Send your tiny shards into the hearts of all in my domain. Take from them the ability to see the good and beautiful things that abide in this world. Make their happiness turn to depression. Make them feel the discouragement they have made me suffer. Freeze their hearts."

The mirror shattered, and the tiny shards lifted into the air. They drifted unnoticed throughout the kingdom as the king collapsed from exhaustion, and his eyes returned to their piercing blue.

Prince Snow was in the village. He had heard of the sudden deaths of many children in the kingdom and felt it was his duty to sympathize with the heartbroken families. Of course, he had no idea that the children had been his own half-siblings, or that his father had ordered their deaths. His kind heart only demanded that he care for those that made the kingdom prosperous.

A lovely young woman, crying beside a newly covered grave, drew his attention. He stopped to mourn with her, saying, "My dear, I understand how badly it hurts to lose someone precious to you. I still cry sometimes over my mother, the queen. She was lost to me far too soon. Was this your child?"

"No, Prince Snow. This was my brother. He was only eight years of age. He never did anyone wrong, yet he was found in the woods with a broken neck. Other children were found in similar circumstances. What has happened? Can you stop it? Will the king find the guilty person and punish them?" the girl begged.

"I know not what my father will do. He has never confided in me. In fact, except for my birthday celebration, he seldom acknowledges my existence. I am sorry for your loss, and the loss of all the other families. I swear I will seek out the guilty one and have him punished. What is your name, my dear?"

"I am Anabelle. My brother was Martin. I shall miss him for the rest of my life," the girl declared.

"As I do my mother," Prince Snow replied. "It is only natural. Come. Walk with me. We shall gaze upon the fields of flowers and smell their wonderful scents. Perhaps, this will ease the sorrows in our hearts."

The prince placed Anabelle's soft, delicate hand upon his arm and began to cross the flower-strewn field. "Why have you shorn your hair?" He dared to ask, for Anabelle's dark locks were chopped off shorter than his own.

"When I was told of Martin's death, I wished to

look as I felt; ugly and in pain. I ripped much of it out with my hands. Mother sympathized with me and she cut off the rest. It will grow as my heartache lessens," she confided.

Prince Snow was enchanted by the soft, innocent heart of Anabelle. He had never met a kinder soul, except for his mother. It was all he could do to keep from planting a kiss on her delectable lips. This was a girl he would consider keeping forever. His loins were tight and tingling to take her virginity. He bent to pick a few flowers to give the girl as a token of his high esteem and missed noticing the tiny, silver sparkle of the frozen shards floating through the air. He let out a gasp as one penetrated his heart but did not understand what caused the pain.

The undeniable happiness he had begun to feel since meeting Anabelle started to quickly dissipate. He first assumed it was because of the sympathy he had for her situation, but it went to a much deeper level than that. As he continued to walk at her side, a sadness developed in his soul. He had a difficult time containing it. Then, an anger he didn't understand took over. Now, instead of seduction, he wished to force a kiss, or more, upon Anabelle.

The prince didn't want the sweet girl to see the change that had come over him. He was confused by the swift downward spiral of his feelings. He suddenly found himself becoming annoyed by the single tear that slipped from her beautiful, gray eyes. He wished to get away; and do so quickly.

"Anabelle," he ground out in a less than kind

voice. "I have business to attend to. I must leave you here."

Without uttering another word, he walked away. His pace quickened considerably as the sky turned darker according to his eyes, and the color of the flowers faded. Even the sweet scent of the meadow was gone, leaving only a nasty smelling odor lingering in the air. He couldn't remember what beauty he had once seen in Anabelle. She was now only a stranger with a broken heart and a wretched haircut. Anger at himself for wasting time consoling her overcame his heart.

This new Prince Snow confused him. He didn't like himself at all. Where had his kind heart disappeared to? What had happened to change him from one moment to the next? The prince was never angry, not even at his hard-hearted father. Though he had his share of women, he would never harm one, or force them to become his mistress. He was always full of love, just like his mother had been before her death. Remembering the day she had been buried, and he hadn't been allowed one final goodbye, he hung his head and cried.

Prince Snow was devastated. No more would he laugh at the jester's jokes, tease the cooks to gain more sweets, or offer aid to those less fortunate. Caring for others or laughing were now beyond his abilities. What was he to do?

*****

Alone in his room the prince lost control. He

smashed an heirloom statue against the stone wall. It shattered all over the floor and crackled beneath his feet as he paced back and forth. He wanted to put his fist through the wall but managed to refrain himself. Instead, he pounded the bed until feathers flew up in the air.

Stopping briefly at the window, Prince Snow caught a glimpse of his father shouting at one of the farmers. Once upon a time he would have rushed out to protect the old man from the king's cruel tongue, but today he was afraid his own words would be harsher than the king's.

Prince Snow vowed to stay hidden in his rooms until the unnatural anger passed. He assumed it would leave him shortly and his demeanor would return to normal. However, when he witnessed the king take a young woman from the farmer's side and drag her to the castle, he felt his hands ball into fists. Worse, he wasn't sure which person he wanted to strangle; his father for forcing a woman to his bed, the old man for allowing his daughter to be taken, or the girl for not fighting harder.

All night he switched from tossing and turning in his bed to pacing the floor and breaking things. As the sun finally rose into the dull gray sky, its light diminished by the darkness in his soul, the prince screamed out, "Why? Someone tell me why?" Then began to pull out his hair and beat his chest.

Bruised and broken, he knew he must be going crazy. He needed help and an explanation. The only person he knew that might understand the anger that was consuming his soul was his own father, the king. After all, King Snow was the angriest, cruelest, and most devious man he had yet encountered.

With his ragged hair standing on end, his face and body covered in scratches, his clothes hanging in strips, and his handsome face ravaged from lack of sleep, the prince sought out his father.

Not recognizing the man that entered the throne room, the king shouted at the guard, "Who is this peasant? I was told my son wished to speak with me. How dare you lie and send in a worthless piece of rubbish!"

"It is me, Father," Prince Snow revealed. "What is happening to me? Help me, please. If there is an ounce of good in you at all, then save me from this evil that has taken over my mind. The world has become dull, plain, and sad. There is no happiness left inside me. I feel only anger and hatred. Tell me what this means!"

King Snow was shocked to see the prince in this horrendous condition. He had expected the spell to cause pain and suffering to those in his kingdom, but he hadn't considered how strong the spell would be. Oddly enough, he was pleased by the destruction his spell had caused. It meant he was more powerful than even he had imagined. He was proud of his accomplishment. This suffering was far better than a quick death would have been.

Unable to keep from bragging, the king told the truth for the first time in his wretched life. "I brought this evil upon you. The spell I cast cannot be broken. You will never see, or feel, the beauty of this world again. It is lost to everyone in this kingdom. It is your own fault. You, Prince Snow, are the reason for this evil. You tried to take my place as the most handsome in the land, and that cannot be allowed. Because you would have then taken the throne, I wanted you dead. My men were too cowardly to take your life, so I cast this spell. You are no longer handsome in the eyes of my people. I will remain the best in the land."

"It was you that had the children killed, wasn't it? Why? What had they done to you?"

King Snow laughed evilly and replied, "Do you not yet understand? Those children were your brothers and sisters. They could not be allowed to grow up and surpass my beautiful countenance. No one must hold out hope to take my place, so they had to die."

"Why did you allow me to live?' Prince Snow asked, horror ripping at his soul for the little ones that were lost to him before he had known they were his kin.

"As I said, my men were too cowardly to cause your death. They were fond of you, you see. I thought about committing the deed myself, but I lost my head in anger. I cast this spell in a moment of complete frustration, and I must admit it has worked out in my favor. The whole kingdom can be held in subjection, and I will make certain you are blamed for everything bad that occurs from this point on. No one will love you, or bow to you, ever again," King Snow declared gleefully.

"All spells can be broken," the prince proclaimed. "You are not a true sorcerer; just a poor imitator. I was once frightened of you when you stated that you were a sorcerer, but I am no longer a child. I will defeat you, and it will be you who dies. The spell has overcome any love I held for you. You, dear Father, have created a monster that is worse than yourself. For that stupidity, you will pay with your ungodly life."

The prince turned his back on the king and stomped from the throne room. He had stood up to his father, but now he deflated. Discouragement took the place of bravado. How could he break a spell that he wasn't privy to? He would need to know the exact spell, how it was cast, and what the antidote was. The task was impossible. It would have been better if the king's men had killed him.

*****

Prince Snow wandered through the village. Gone were the laughing, jolly ones who usually occupied the fruit stalls, giving away apples or peaches to hungry children. In their place were steely-eyed men who watched the throngs for any signs of thievery. The hungry children were knocked to the ground or the guards were called to take them away. Prince Snow did not intervene.

There was no joyful singing as the women washed their clothing in the river's depth. Instead, they argued over the smallest imagined transgression. One woman fell into the river and was swept away by the rushing water. No one lifted a finger to save her, not even the prince.

A knife fight broke out at the butcher's shop. When Prince Snow began to chant along with the crowd, "Slice his belly open!", the hatred he felt for himself exceeded its limits. The only way to stop this madness was to die. He couldn't be the cause of any of his subjects being beheaded for killing him, so he must do the deed all by himself.

All week he considered what would be the easiest and most successful way to destroy himself. Poison was too painful and not easy to get when everyone knew you were the prince. He thought about a hangman's noose, but he knew the rope could break, and he might be left alive and addlebrained. A knife to his heart, or drowning were his best choices.

It was more difficult than the prince expected to overcome his deep depression and make a wise decision to take his own life. There was a small piece inside him that fought to live. Perhaps, if he combined a stab to his chest with a drowning in the swift moving river, he would succeed.

He found a lonely stretch of the river where the current was particularly fast. It also had the benefit of being hidden by large trees and brush. Here, he began to undress. His doublet, shirt, and boots were already discarded when a soft voice rose from the trees.

"My prince, what are you doing? You cannot swim here. You will certainly drown. The river spins in circles at this spot, sinking all that goes in,"

Anabelle admonished.

"That is the idea, Anabelle. I am here to stop my insanity." The prince drew his knife and held it against his heaving, muscular chest. "I will stab my heart and fall into the river to be washed beneath its waters. I will find peace only in death."

Anabelle's hand flew to her mouth upon hearing the prince's declaration. "You cannot!" she shouted. "Why would you wish this upon yourself? The kingdom needs you. Can't you see there is trouble here? You are needed to end the sadness in our land. The king obviously doesn't wish to help."

"I am the reason for the sadness. It was his anger at me that caused the king to put a spell on our people. He wants me dead, so I will give him what he desires. Perhaps then, he will lift the curse. I cannot stand the sadness and pain any longer. Death is preferable," the prince argued.

"Death is never the correct choice. It is the one unbreakable spell. Once you are gone, you cannot come back," Anabelle replied, reaching out for the knife.

"Stand back!" The prince shouted. "I do not want to cause you harm, but I will if you get in my way. I am wicked and evil. My soul is twisted into something I do not recognize. Do you know that I came very close to taking you without your permission? I would have ravaged you without really knowing you. Don't you see how bad I've become?"

"My sweet, Prince Snow, you could have had me without asking. You are a kind hearted man who cares about this kingdom. I can see your soul, and it is unchanged. I would give myself freely to you in order to prove it, for I have loved you since I was a mere child. Come, let me ease your pain," Anabelle begged.

Shocked and disturbed by her admission, the prince backed away. He stumbled at the edge of the water and almost fell in. Anabelle grabbed for him and pulled him to safety. In doing this good deed, she managed to get cut by the knife. Blood dripped from her arm, startling the prince into forgetting about his mission. He dropped the knife, fell to his knees, and examined the cut on Anabelle's forearm.

To his relief, the cut was shallow, though long. Her thick sleeves had protected Anabelle well. The prince carefully washed the blood away, then wrapped the injury in a piece of cloth torn from his discarded shirt.

"Why would you risk yourself to save a wretched fool like me?" Prince Snow asked.

"I still see the beauty inside you. My innocent heart has not been touched by the king's spell. I see the good. Love gave me the strength to save you. Please, Prince Snow, let me help end the spell and the king's reign. Together, we can conquer whatever obstacles we come across."

Prince Snow's head tilted as he stared into Anabelle's lovely eyes. He saw truth there and a small glimpse of the beauty that was missing in the kingdom.

His lips dropped to hers, and when they touched, a spark of hope developed in his soul.

*****

The spark of hope felt so wonderful that Prince Snow couldn't contain his desire. He wanted, no, he needed, more from Anabelle. He pulled her closer, careful not to cause unnecessary pain to her injured arm. She allowed the closeness, giving all the beauty she could still see and feel back to the prince. He reveled in the wonder of her innocent love. The emotions she emitted took hold in his soul, and he wasn't sure if he would be able to stop with just a few kisses.

The prince gasped and pulled away, shoving Anabelle gently away. He exclaimed, "I'm sorry, but I couldn't help myself. If I don't end this now, I won't be able to keep from going too far. You are an innocent. It would be a travesty to force myself on you."

"It wouldn't be force. I want you to take me. I will give myself freely, as you are the man I love. There has never been another that I've loved, nor will there ever be. Let me give you the solace you need. Once I have reached your soul, perhaps you will agree to fight the king for the rulership of the kingdom. Everyone needs you, Prince Snow. I need you most of all," Anabelle admitted as she breached the space between them, cupped his ravaged face in her delicate hands, and kissed him as if there was no tomorrow.

Prince Snow groaned. The love Anabelle poured into the sweet kiss sent pain running through his veins. Its honesty and beauty battled against the evil lurking inside him. The kiss proved to be too much to resist. The prince circled Anabelle's body with his strong arms and tumbled to the ground. His tongue pushed at her lips, and she obligingly opened her mouth to the intrusion.

She tasted of honey, strawberries, and sunshine. Prince Snow's heart pounded against his chest, trying desperately to hold on to the spell the king had cast. The prince closed his eyes to hide Anabelle's lovely face from his view, but the love she gave him continued to grow.

Soft hands roamed his hard, sculpted chest. One stilled over his pounding heart and then was replaced by Anabelle's soft lips. The prince came alive with that gentle kiss. He frantically tore at Anabelle's clothing, eliciting a moan of pleasure from her when he was able to put his lips over a bare breast.

Anabelle bowed her back, lifting her chest toward Prince Snow's suckling mouth, silently telling him she liked what was happening. A smile, something he thought could never occur again, crossed his lips before he moved to the other plump, rounded mound.

"Oh, my love, I have dreamed of this moment," Anabelle sighed.

The confession made the prince bolder. His hands slid down the folds of her dress, gathering the material as they lowered toward her legs.

Anabelle either didn't notice, or she didn't care, that the prince would soon be touching her bare skin where no man had ever touched her before.

She was busy doing her own exploring. Her fingers grazed the taut nipples on his proud chest. He whimpered but continued his trail down her body. Anabelle's hand moved downward and ran across the rippled muscles of his abdomen. Her fingers eventually were stopped by the intrusion of cloth, the pants the prince still wore. A tiny spark of fear mixed with her desire. She had an idea of what was hidden beneath the cloth. She had seen what happened between animals, and her mother had once explained how babies were made.

The fear disappeared as if by magic the moment Prince Snow's large hand touched her naked thigh. A tingling need took its place. A dampness at the apex of her thighs announced her desire. It was obvious that the prince desired her as well. The thick staff she felt against her leg grew harder and longer. It seemed to be pulsing. Her own dampness grew in answer to the staff's call.

Prince Snow gulped in air. He tried to slow down his heartbeat and his desire, but the scent of Anabelle's need was too much to handle. It broke through his resolve to stop before taking her innocence. His thumb caressed the center of her thighs, and her body leapt with pleasure. He tentatively moved his thumb in circles over the nub he found. He watched Anabelle's face contort in question. She was confused by what she was feeling.

"It is fine, dear Anabelle. This is how it is supposed to feel. Relax, and let the feeling flow through you."

Anabelle obeyed the prince's command. The beautiful agony came quickly. She lost sight of Prince Snow's face, seeing only stars circling across her eyelids. How had she not known such pleasure existed? Her hips bucked, hoping the sensation would never cease. A single tear slid down her cheek.

Prince Snow saw the tear and faltered. He began to move off Anabelle, afraid he had harmed her, or that she regretted allowing his touch.

"No! Don't leave me. I am not hurt. The tear was nothing but joy. Please, finish what you started. Your needs have not been met," Anabelle soothed.

Oddly, Prince Snow wasn't concerned about his own needs. Anabelle's happiness was all he wanted. If she demanded him to go on, and she was feeling joy, then so be it.

The prince shed his pants and hovered above her. He asked one more time, "Are you certain this is what you want?"

Anabelle smiled and replied, "More than life itself."

Prince Snow kept his eyes on Anabelle's as he slowly slid inside her tight tunnel. Her eyes widened, then began to glow. Her expression spoke of love so true that the prince forgot he was ever doubtful of her desire or his own. This felt right.

Once he had filled her, he began to move. Surprise crossed her face. He supposed she hadn't realized the tension could build once more, and she would be able to lose herself in pleasure a second time. He shocked himself by wanting to give her that gift and slowed his movements to allow for it. His own gratification would come soon enough.

Anabelle's mouth formed a silent 'O' when she lost herself again. Prince Snow grinned and lost control. He pounded his way to satisfaction, then collapsed upon the limp body of Anabelle.

Anabelle grunted and shoved at his shoulders. He was heavy, and she was unable to breathe properly, though she would be happy if she died beneath the prince. She truly had loved him all her life, and if this moment in time was all she ever got of him, then that would be enough to sustain her forever.

When Prince Snow sat up, understanding Anabelle's need for air, he felt a tingling near his eye. As he reached up to touch it, Anabelle grabbed his hand to stop him.

"Wait! Let me see what it is," she demanded.

The teardrop sparkled. It was silver, which didn't seem natural to Anabelle. It slid slowly down Prince Snow's cheek. She carefully let it land on her fingertip, then let out a gasp. "Snow, my love! It is not a tear. It is a shard of glass, a piece of a mirror."

Not caring that Anabelle had shortened his name, and spoke to him in such familiar tones, the prince stared blankly at the broken piece of mirror she held out for him to see.

"The spell you spoke of; how was it formed?" Anabelle asked.

"Father's magic mirrors," the prince replied in awe. "He uses them to cast spells. He is not a real sorcerer. He cannot do spells without their aid."

"Look at me, Snow. Has the world changed yet again? Can you see its beauty? Is the sadness gone?" She inquired.

Prince Snow glanced at the trees. They were bright green. The sky was no longer gray. It was blue, and the sun was bright once more. Anabelle's face was the most beautiful of all. Happiness filled his heart and soul where Anabelle now dwelled.

"I see everything clearly, dear Anabelle. How did this happen?" The prince wished to know.

"Our innocent love broke the spell. The mirrors cannot stop love. They don't understand the concept. Neither does your father. You are free. We must visit the enchantress who lives in the deepest part of the woods. She will know how to help the others. Your father's treachery must end."

"I swear I will stop his evil or die in the process. Take me to the enchantress," Prince Snow declared.

*****

"You should go alone," Anabelle told the prince. "I'll spy on the king. He will soon realize that the spell on you has been broken. If he has had your brothers and sisters killed, then surely he will continue to seek your death. I can be there to hear his commands or stop him."

"That is not a safe plan. He can destroy you. Not only is he twisted enough to harm you on his own, but he has the power of the magic mirrors at his beckoning," Prince Snow warned.

"True, it is not safe, but it must be done this

way. The king's secrets cannot remain hidden. The entire kingdom will be destroyed if his evil plans are brought to fruition. Let me do this one thing to save our kingdom. Let me prove that I am worthy of your love," Anabelle beseeched.

Prince Snow reluctantly agreed. He memorized the directions to the enchantress's home, then watched as Anabelle disappeared through the trees. He frowned in concern, wanting to forget about his trip to see the enchantress and follow the woman he now knew he loved, to protect her from his evil father. However, he also knew that he had no power over the magic his father had control of, so to defeat the king he would need the help of the enchantress's magic.

He began to run, following the almost invisible markings on the trees that Anabelle had promised would guide him to his destination. The faster he got to the enchantress, the sooner he could be back to protect Anabelle.

He stopped abruptly when he stumbled into a clearing. It was magnificent. There were an abundant number of colorful flowers, some he had never seen in all his life. A mountain that should not have existed in this kingdom stood over a stone cottage. Water cascaded from the waterfall in the mountain's center. Prince Snow was stunned by the beauty before him, but confused as to where this unusual place could have come from, and why he couldn't hear the gushing waterfall.

A voice came to his ears through the soft breeze. "You are the young prince. I have been waiting for you. You may enter my domain."

Prince Snow made one careful step out of the shadows and into the sunlight. His skin tingled as he walked through an invisible barrier. Once inside, he could hear the waterfall, the birds singing, and smell the aroma of the flowers. It was magic that had hidden this domain from him all his life. He doubted the king knew of its existence.

The most beautiful woman he had ever seen stepped from the cottage. Her long hair flowed gently in the breeze. Tiny flowers were woven into the tresses. A soft dress of white floated over the enchantress's body, all the way to her delicate feet. When her eyes met the prince's, he saw swirls of stars amidst their blue orbs.

"You are too young to be the enchantress I am seeking," Prince Snow stuttered.

"Looks are deceiving. As your father's beauty hides an evil soul, mine is an illusion to hide the ancient visage of my body and face. Why should I be wrinkled and shriveled when I have the power to remain lovely? If you have come to me, then things in the kingdom have reached a distressing point. What has the king done?" The enchantress asked.

"Don't you know? Haven't you felt the change in our world?" Prince Snow inquired. "You have magic, so you should be aware of the disturbance in the surroundings. You should have sensed the evil in the air."

"Once upon a time I might have, but when your father became king, I shut myself off from the kingdom. His evilness was too much to bear. I made this domain to protect myself, and have not stepped out of it in many years. I knew that someday, you would come to seek me out. The end of King Snow's reign of terror must be approaching."

"Father thinks he is a sorcerer. He has used the power of one of his mirrors to cast a spell on the kingdom's people. They can no longer see beauty or good in the world. Everything appears dull. All the people are sad, or angry. Love has disappeared. Father also had his henchmen kill every illegitimate offspring he sired. Death has brought more sadness to permeate the kingdom. I was trapped in his spell, until the love of an innocent girl reached my soul and broke through the evil. We need your help," the prince explained.

"Ah, then he found them. The mirrors were a gift from me to one of your ancestors; a king who ruled with love a hundred years ago. Each king to come after him has used them only for good. When your father was born, his evil spirit became visible to me. The mirrors warned your grandfather of the treacherous soul within his son. Together, we hid the mirrors so that your father could never use them against anyone. I hid myself to keep him from torturing me into disclosing their hiding place. It was all for nothing, since he has clearly found them anyway. This was my mistake, and it is I who must fix it. It is time for me to reappear," the enchantress answered.

While Prince Snow was speaking to the enchantress, Anabelle had entered the castle. She was surprised when no guards appeared to stop her.

One stood weeping in a corner, while another gazed up at nothing. The spell was growing stronger. The guards were suffering from sadness, or indifference.

Anabelle made her way to the king's chambers. She could hear murmurings from behind the closed door, but the words were unintelligible. Carefully, she pushed the door open just a tiny bit. She hoped to catch the king making evil plans against her sweet Snow.

Suddenly, the door was jerked from her grasp. She could not stop the momentum of her body, and fell to the floor at the king's feet.

"Well, what have we here?" King Snow asked the mirrors, which were now standing around his chamber instead of hidden in the secret room. "Have I been sent a gift to entertain me?"

A mirror spoke, "To the handsome prince the girl belongs. For the king to touch her would be wrong."

"Shut up!" The king shouted. "She has come to my chamber, so she is my plaything. When the prince comes, he will find nothing that resembles a woman."

"Prince Snow will defeat you," Anabelle dared to utter. "I will not give in to your magic. You are not a sorcerer."

The king growled in anger, and commanded, "Seal her mouth. Do not let her speak. Words must never leave her mouth. It is silence I seek."

Light sprang from one of the mirrors. It reached Anabelle's lips, and the burning it caused brought great pain. Anabelle fought against it, refusing to collapse. Though her mouth was charred, it was not sealed. She managed to taunt the king, "You will lose this battle. If you have no power over a peasant, then you cannot defeat the prince."

Furious, King Snow flung her to the floor. He kicked her and screamed with all his might, "Shrivel to half your size! A dead plant will be your disguise."

Agony shot through Anabelle's arms and legs. They grew thinner, the muscles shriveling to almost nothing. Yet, she remained a human. She was scarred, but still beautiful. "You are not strong enough to destroy me. The mirrors no longer give their full power to you. Their loyalty is switching to your son," Anabelle scoffed.

Outraged by her words, the king gave in to his evil desires. He lifted Anabelle from the floor and tossed her wilted body onto the bed. "If I cannot change what you are, I can ruin you for my son. I will sire a son with you, and destroy the prince. Then, I will have the power of the mirrors once more."

King Snow began ripping at Anabelle's clothes. He bared her body to his lecherous eyes. His spells had left it untouched. Her curves were still beautiful, bringing lust to the king's soul. He hardened against her thigh.

As the king began to tear at his pants, the door burst open once more. Prince Snow grabbed the king by the hair and slung him against the wall. The prince's anger, and his love for Anabelle, gave him the strength and courage of an army.

The handful of hair he had torn from the king's head fell to the floor. The king, stunned but still conscious, tried to attack, wrapping his arms around the prince's legs. Prince Snow lifted the larger man into the air as if he was nothing, and tossed him toward the mirrors. He landed with a thud, slamming his head into the floor.

"You will die for daring to touch Anabelle," Prince Snow roared. He lifted a chair and was about to bring it down on his father's head when Anabelle shouted.

"Snow! Do not kill him. It will make you as evil as he is. Let him rot in prison."

"He has too much power. He will break out and destroy us all. The mirrors will help him," The prince declared.

"Not anymore. They don't complete his bidding. He has only the partial use of their power now, otherwise I would have lost the ability to speak, and I would be a dead, shriveled plant. The mirrors are yours, I think," she explained.

*****

"Partial power is still too much. Look at you, my love. He has scarred you," Prince Snow replied.

"Am I not still beautiful to you, Snow?" Anabelle cried out.

"Forever beautiful, my dear," the prince swore.

Noise from the courtyard reached their ears. The enchantress had arrived, and she was chanting a spell to counteract the king's evil one.

Snow dragged his father to the balcony, his arm across the king's throat. Wrapped in the bedding to hide her bare form, Anabelle followed. Beneath the balcony stood the beautiful enchantress. Her arms were raised to the sky, and she was causing the clouds to darken.

"Wash away the mistakes that evil made. Return the kingdom to the way it used to be. Show the king's true nature. May love's power bring beauty back for all to see," she chanted.

Rain cascaded from the sky. It was not the usual rain, but one filled with love potion. The pink drops fell upon the anxious raised faces of the people of the land. Their expressions began to change. Smiles replaced frowns. Tears became laughter. The spell was breaking.

The king's shrill shrieks echoed off the trees. He struggled against Prince Snow's hold. The enchantress turned her eyes toward him, and scowled. She shouted out over the cheering crowd. "You were never worthy to be king. I should have destroyed you at birth, but if I had your son would never have been born. It has been foretold that he and his love, Anabelle, will rule this kingdom with the love it deserves, and bring forth generations of sons to keep it perfect. Your existence was necessary for the prophecy to be fulfilled."

The king began to writhe in Prince Snow's arms. He shouted words of command to the mirrors, but could not be heard over the gleeful shouts of the crowd. He lost control and his words became insane rantings.

Prince Snow looked at the enchantress for instructions. She nodded her head and bowed to him, understanding what he wished to do. Without speaking, Snow and Anabelle rushed inside and broke all the mirrors. With each piece that shattered, the king screamed in pain. No more could the mirrors be used for evil purposes. Their magic dissipated in the wind. Snow and Anabelle did not need them to rule the kingdom. Their magic came from their hearts, and the love they shared.

Anabelle's lips healed as the mirrors broke. Her arms and legs became strong once more. The hair she had ripped out after her brother's death grew back. The long dark locks curled invitingly over her pale skin.

The king's appearance began to change as well. Where his thick hair had been, there were now wispy strands of white. His face contorted to match his evil soul. His shoulders hunched, and his legs twisted. He was hideous to look upon. He was revealed to his people as an ugly beast, his outside now equal to his treacherous soul.

"You are hereby banished from this kingdom," Prince Snow commanded the beast. "Alone, you will wander the world; untouched and unloved by anyone. Your power is gone along with the mirrors. We need never fear you again."

The hideous beast that the king had become, crawled from the castle and into the woods. The people of the land pelted him with stones, their hatred for him apparent in their faces. The enchantress blinded his eyes to the road back to the kingdom. She made certain he would never find his way back.

Snow was now the king, and soon Anabelle would be his queen.

Of Rose and Thorn
Channie Cocker

Queen Louanna longs to give her King an heir, but finds herself barren. In her despair, she cries out to anyone that might hear her plea and begs for a way to get pregnant. A tiny frog offers a way to make this possible, and in her desperation, Louanna is eager to accept, no matter what the cost may be. Nightmares ensue and she seeks the favor of the fairies to protect her child. This sick and twisted tale will shock you and leave you longing for more!

The queen stared outside her window with longing. She watched as a beautiful young maiden had fallen into labor and was being escorted to the midwife's cottage. The father stood outside pacing and waiting eagerly. The queen knew she should be overjoyed for the young maiden, but alas, she was fraught with jealousy and rage. The king deserved to have such a moment as that young man did down below.

"That should be me down there. Not her," she whispered.

"My Queen, your time shall come," the king encouraged. She turned to her husband and sighed deeply. "Truly, I hope your words are right, but I fear they are not. The whole country now calls me barren. Could there be no greater insult? What is a queen if she cannot give her king an heir? I have done nothing but bring you shame," she moaned pitifully. The king walked up to her and wrapped his arms around her with pure affection.

"My dearest Louanna, you have brought me nothing but sunshine and happiness. I shall love you always, no matter what words may be thrown at us." His words flowed like honey and soothed her aching soul. She leaned into him, and for a time, she was content.

*****

Louanna sat forlornly by the pond as she dipped her hand into the water and filled the pond more with her unstoppable tears. Was she the only maiden who did not bear a child? Could it be that she had been cursed? Maybe it was time to suggest to the king that he should get a concubine. The very thought tore at the depths of her heart and she immediately dismissed the idea. Looking into the pond water, she watched as the water rippled.

"I wish... no, I pray... I beg... please give me a child! I'll do anything!" She cried. Just then, a frog hopped out of the pond and landed in her lap. She let out a tiny squeal before she managed to compose herself.

The frog looked up at her imploringly. He was a small bright green frog with large blue eyes popping out of his head. They didn't seem like frog eyes, but had a more human quality about them. Louanna found it very intriguing and somewhat familiar. It waited there calmly for a few moments then let out a loud croak.

"You will have a daughter. However, there is one thing you must do," the frog spoke.

"What is it, tiny frog?" Louanna begged, not caring that this frog could talk.

"You must mix my seed in with the King's seed. That is the only way," the frog stated simply as though it were not a big deal. The queen was disgusted by the very thought and looked away quickly.

"I do not think I could do such a thing," she admitted.

"You said you would do anything. Well, this is what you must do," he croaked. She looked down at him and wondered, was it worth it?

"How would I do this thing you ask of me?" She whispered.

"You will know when the time comes. This is our secret. You cannot tell anyone," he warned. It was tempting to laugh at this tiny amphibian looking so serious.

"Who would believe it of me? A talking frog? I scarcely believe it myself," she chuckled lightly.

The frog croaked irritably before hopping back into the water. Louanna watched the ripples fade away before sitting up straight and pondering what the frog had demanded of her. She had to resolve to do as the frog asked. It was the only way to procure a daughter. Surely it would not be that difficult, right? She quickly put such thoughts out of her mind as she imagined what her daughter would look like.

She would have her father's eyes and her mother's full red lips. She would be lithe and sing like an angel. These were the things that she longed for in her child. Images of her daughter went from dream to nightmare immediately. She saw her daughter swaying in a field with huge bug eyes and instead of singing with the voice of an angel, she croaked like a frog. It was more than Louanna could bear. She stood and walked briskly out of the courtyard and on to her bed chambers. She suddenly felt ill and needed to lie down. Those whom she passed by knew not to speak to her as they saw the storms brewing in her eyes, and were not to disturb her in such a state.

Louanna woke to pressure on her backside. An arm reached around and cupped her breast and a fully erect cock pressed harder against her. She moaned with pleasure as the king nibbled her ear. Soon they were in the throes of lovemaking as he entered her with such ferocity that it caused her to cry out. The king was none the wiser as her next cry was louder but not from his ministrations, but rather at the sight of the small frog sitting near their gyrating hips. Large mucous like pustules formed on his back. In her mind she heard the familiar voice of the frog say, 'Take my seed. Now is the time. Mix it with the king's and you shall have your heir!'

She closed her eyes and forced herself to believe she was reaching for the king's massive member. She scooped up the glob of mucous then reached in to insert it inside of her. The frog watched as she succeeded in doing as he commanded. A morbid laugh echoed in her mind as the frog slowly faded away. Though the frog was gone, Louanna felt his presence linger and knew that he was watching them. The King opened his eyes and looked down at her inquisitively. It was then that she realized she still had her hand inside her. To avoid questions, she forced a playful smirk on her face and started to rub his manhood. Completely turned on by her sudden boldness he entered faster and harder. She moved her hand just before it got pommeled by his burst of excitement. Their release was glorious, and by the end, they were completely spent. The pleasure of it lingered through her body, coursing through her and blotting out the frog's part in all of it. She slept well that night, the first night in ages.

*****

"My Queen! You are with child!" The midwife declared as she felt around Louanna's stomach. She had her suspicions since she had gotten sick every morning for weeks now. Her heart beat with joy at the words of the midwife. She was indeed with child and it was the most amazing news she could imagine.

"Go! Tell the King! This is most fortuitous news!" Louanna commanded. The midwife lifted up her skirts and darted out of the room as fast as her short legs could go. She had been the castle midwife for many generations and was highly respected. What seemed like minutes passed before the king came waltzing into the room, the joy evident on his face as the corners of his mouth touched from ear to ear. Even after so many years Louanna still found him to be the most handsome man in the realm.

"Tell me it's true!" The king demanded.

"Rowan, it is true. I am with child," Louanna cried out with joy. Rowan leaned down and gave his beloved a gentle squeeze. She knew he wanted to be very careful, and she did not blame him one bit for it, for she wanted to do the same.

"We must prepare a celebration!" He exclaimed. Yes, it would do the kingdom well to have such excellent news. He kissed her brow before leaving the room hastily in his excitement.

"That man is still so much a boy," the midwife teased as she helped Louanna get comfortable on the bed.

"Oh, good mother, he is very much a man. He's just excited," the queen laughed. Her mind was suddenly filled with thoughts of her husband's naked body causing shivers of delight to coarse through her body and heat up her core. Her thighs and mound ached for his touch.

"You both are still children to me. I helped bring both of you into this world," she winked.

"That you did. And now you will help bring my little babe into this world as well," Louanna laughed despite the midwife's words breaking her spell of longing.

The midwife came over and tucked Louanna into bed, making sure all her needs were being met. Louanna appreciated the special attention. Everyone wanted to ensure the safety and health of this baby. She would not complain. The midwife left her to sleep then so she could start the new day fresh and well rested. There was much to prepare for, and she needed to be ready to face her people. They would all be wanting to see her to know that the words were true. She lay there for some time before drifting off to sleep. Her mind raced with all the things that had occurred throughout the day. Soon she was sleeping soundly and fell into a dark dream.

*****

She lay in her bed with her legs propped up. She was crying out for Rowan due to the immense pain her body was going through. The only words were from the midwife who was giving her directions to breath and push. Each push was even more agonizing. She finally gave one last hard push and was soon met with not cries but frog croaks instead. The midwife shrieked as she quickly handed the babe to its mother and left the room screaming. At first, Louanna was distracted by the midwife's behavior, but soon looked down upon the baby in her arms. She about screamed herself at the sight before her. Her tiny bundle had large bulbous eyes that popped out of her face and her hands and feet were webbed. When the wee one looked up at her with those big eyes, she let out a loud croak, causing the queen to scream.

Louanna woke from the dream with the scream escaping her lips. Maids, midwife, guards, and the King all came running in to check on her. When she was able to gain her bearings, she explained that she had a bad dream and it was nothing to worry about. Just the fears that come with being an expectant mother. Relieved, everyone left to go back to sleep or their duties. Louanna lay in bed for some time with that dream mulling over in her mind. She did not want her child to wind up looking like that and knew that it was very possible to wind up that way. She had to think of something fast. Who could she turn to to ensure that her darling babe did not wind up looking like that?

It was customary for the fairies of the land to come and give their blessing to children about to be born in royalty. Their blessing was said to have kept the kingdom at peace and safe for many lifetimes. And often their blessings came to be just as they were foretold. No one dared to thwart a fairy's blessing. It would bring bad luck to the kingdom. Louanna wondered if it were possible to beg of the fairies to bless her child with very specific blessings. If they could bless her with things such as beauty, grace, and a beautiful singing voice, well that would ensure her daughter would not become the frog like creature that she feared she might be. She would have to be quick and secretive about this. It would not be in her favor should anyone discover what she was about to do.

Louanna got up, wrapped her cloak tightly about her, and took the secret passage through the castle to escape unnoticed. Not many people knew of this passage which made it the wiser choice in this matter. She moved swiftly away from the castle as she glided down the hillside and into the dense forest below. There, she could summon the fairies and hope they give her favor. She entered the woods and quickly fell on bent knee.

"Dearest Fae, I beseech thee. I beg an audience of thee," the queen sang out. Before her bowed head many twinkling lights appeared and hovered just above her before materializing right in front of her.

"Our queen, what is it you seek of us?" The sing song voice of the fairy had a beautiful magical quality to it that caused the hairs on Louanna's arms to stand on end.

"If you would be so kind, I ask that you allow me to tell you what kind of blessings I would like to be spoken over my child." The queen dared not look up for fear of being rejected.

"This is a most unusual request. Might we inquire to the nature of it?" the fairy queried.

"I have been riddled with nightmares that she will be hideous to look upon and that her voice would be pain to the ears. I could not bear that my child would be scorned in such a way. I had hoped that your blessings would ensure this does not happen to her," the queen explained with heartfelt tears. The fairies looked upon her with pity.

"Rise dear queen. We will grant your request. It is true you will have a daughter and we want the very best for her and the kingdom. Tell us what blessings you wish us to bestow upon this fair child? When the time is right, we will appear before the court and place our blessings."

The queen stood tall and proud. Never had she felt so bold as she spoke the words she would have declared over her child. There was no doubt in her mind that these things would come to pass, and the fear of what evils might be bestowed upon her or her child were soon squelched in the light of these blessings.

The fairies rejoiced with her, not once thinking that even they could be deceived.

*****

Louanna gave birth to her daughter with little pain. Though her entire focus had been on her labor, she did catch a frog looking through the window upon the child that had now been removed from her birth canal. He disappeared once the first cries had been heard.

"Congratulations, my Queen! It is a girl!" The midwife declared.

"Aurora, Princess of the Briar," the Queen announced.

The midwife cleaned and bundled the babe then handed her to the queen. Louanna feared looking upon her child and had to force herself to peek at the bundle in her arms. Taking a deep breath, she looked down into the beautiful face of her daughter. Her sky-blue eyes stared upon her mother as she gave out a tiny cry. She had a cute upturned nose and rosy red cheeks. Her eyes were large, but did not bulge out like a frog's, much to the queen's relief. The babe cried out again only much louder this time.

"My Queen, I do believe the babe is hungry," the midwife winked.

"Oh, of course," Louanna blushed as she moved Aurora to her teat to suckle. She had considered a wet nurse, but turned the thought down since she was not sure she would ever have a child again. The princess was now content as she fed hungrily from her mother's bosom.

"Shall I inform the king my lady?" The midwife asked.

"Yes, please do," Louanna replied softly as she

watched her daughter with a contented sigh.

The midwife left the room to fetch the king, leaving the queen alone with her daughter. Louanna fell fast asleep with the princess still at her teat. The exhaustion had taken its toll on her and she could no longer keep herself awake. After what seemed mere minutes, she was woken by a loud croak nearby. Louanna opened her eyes to find the frog looking at her with mournful eyes.

"Dear heavens! Don't just pop up like that! You will frighten the child," Louanna declared.

"I am most sorry, dear. I only wished to see our daughter," the frog replied calmly.

"Our daughter?" Louanna raised a delicate brow.

"She is just as much a part of me as she is of you and the King. Or had you forgotten?" the frog said as he tilted his head.

"No, of that I surely have not forgotten," Louanna stated softly.

"I wish to be a part of her life," the frog whispered as his long tongue forked out and touched the babe's head. The action made Louanna want to faint.

"I do not think that would be wise!" She declared.

"You would deny me this right?" The frog asked, anger rising.

"I would," Louanna said boldly.

"You will regret this," the frog threatened before vanishing in thin air.

Louanna's heart beat wildly as she looked about

the room for any sign of the frog. Her fear ebbed slightly when he was nowhere to be found. She adjusted Aurora so she could feed off the other teat and get her fill. Louanna wanted her to be healthy and strong. The frog's sudden appearance and disappearance had disturbed her greatly and she feared yet again for her child. Aurora fell fast asleep after she'd had her fill and pulled from her mother's bosom, leaving Louanna's breasts fully exposed.

The king walked in at that moment with a mischievous grin on his face. The queen was too tired to notice that he had taken the babe from her arms and handed her to the midwife to take to the nursery. There would be a wet nurse there just to give his beloved a break from time to time. Now was such a time. He kissed his beautiful daughter on the forehead before she was taken out. Once the room was empty, he walked up to his wife's bed and leaned down low over her. Grabbing both large breasts in his hands he stuck his face in between them. Louanna opened her tired eyes to find her husband's face in her bosom, causing her to chuckle. Her laugh emboldened him as his lips sought her taut nipple and sucked vigorously. Louanna gasped as the pleasure of his sucking flowed through her tired body.

Knowing that it would be a while before he could consummate with his beloved again, he decided to take advantage of the moment as he undid his trousers and whipped out his large cock. He placed it between her full firm breasts and held them tightly against his member as he leveled himself above her to keep balance. His gyrating motions between her breasts caused her to let out a moan. She lifted her neck and brought the tip of his cock into her mouth, sucking it as vigorously as he had sucked on her nipples. Now was his turn to moan as she continued to suck. She was tired, but knew he needed the release and wanted nothing more than to please him.

The king's seed spilled into her mouth and coated her throat. The amount of the seemingly constant flow caused her to swallow several times before finally she lapped up the last of his salty goodness. He carefully lifted himself off of his queen and redid his trousers. A contented smile was plastered on his lips as he looked lovingly upon his wife.

"We must keep this quiet between us. We don't want to cause anyone alarm for our lack of decency," he teased.

"Ah yes, we have to keep up our appearances," Louanna laughed. "I hear the midwife coming. You should leave and allow me to rest. I'm sure our little Rose will need to suckle again soon."

"She is a lucky one," he quipped.

"Be gone you goose," the Queen shooed.

He left her alone then. Alone to ponder how things would go within the next week. They would give her a week to heal and care for her little one. After that she was expected to make a royal appearance in the throne room where they announce the name of the princess and allow the fairies to place their blessings. Louanna would not rest easy until they placed their blessings. Once that was done then she would know her child would be safe.

She drifted off to sleep as the midwife came in to check on her. The midwife knew that the Queen needed to rest so she had kept little Rose in the nursery to allow the Queen the chance to sleep. The midwife tidied up around the room as best as she could, doing her best not to wake the sleeping woman. Soon enough the babe will want to nurse and the midwife knew that the Queen would do better suckling the babe after a good rest.

*****

Louanna sat on her throne next to the King in the throne room. Little Rose nestled snugly into the crook of her arm and was content. The room filled quickly with the subjects of their kingdom. Everyone in the realm was invited to be a part of this historical moment. Those from other kingdoms came far and wide to share in the joy as well. It was a festive and joyous occasion, and no one wanted to miss out on it.

Those that entered stood on the right or left of the thrones to leave room for the fairies' arrival. The fairies entered single file and soon stood before the king and queen. They all bowed slightly to honor them which pleased the royal couple immensely. The king held a hand out in a gesture for the room to be quiet. A hush fell upon the room immediately as everyone eagerly awaited what came next.

The king stood and took a step forward. "My loyal subjects! Today is the day we come together and bring forth the naming of our beautiful princess! Thus, proceeds the blessings of the fairies after. I beg of you to remain silent as we continue our traditions. After all is done then we invite all of you to join us in a royal celebration feast!"

The crowd cheered wildly at the invitation until the king silenced them again. He turned to his queen and motioned for her to stand by his side. She stood eloquently all while holding onto her babe with the care that only comes from a mother. When she stood next to the king he reached over and took his daughter from her and lifted her up for everyone in the room to see.

"I introduce you to your new princess Rose of the house of Briar!" The king bellowed loudly.

They cheered again then all went silent as they watched the king lower Rose into his arms. He looked down upon her with open admiration, proud of his beautiful child. The fairies lined up and were ready to bestow their blessings upon little Rose. He looked up at them and smiled brightly.

"Let the blessings begin!" He announced.

There were five fairies in all and each of them stood tall and proud wearing no clothes. Each one was a different skin tone with matching hair and eyes. Their wings were silver and touched the ground when they stood still. Though the realm was used to seeing the fairies there was still many a roaming eye from the men and several women slapping their husbands for it. The fairies did not allow such things to concern them. They had more important business to attend to.

The red fairy walked up to the king and queen and placed her hands upon the cheeks of the child. She leaned in and placed a gentle kiss upon the babe's lips.

"My blessing is this, that your lips will be as red as blood and your cheeks will always be rosy. May you always love and be loved and offer love to all the land!" A warm red light flowed through the fairy's hands and absorbed into Rose's face. The fairy then removed her hands and backed away.

Next up was the blue fairy. She placed her thumbs on Rose's eyes and said, "My blessing is this, that you will have the most beautiful blue eyes, large and innocent. May you always see the good in others and offer hope to all the land!" A blue light moved from her thumbs into Rose's eyes.

Rose seemed to be very content with what the fairies were doing and allowed them to place their blessings without any dispute. The king and queen were much relieved by this. Next up was the yellow fairy. She placed her hands on the top of Rose's head.

"My blessing is this, that your hair will be the color of the sun and may it always flow long and healthy. May you be a ray of sunshine to those around you and bring warmth to all the land!" A flash of yellow light flowed through Rose's hair and it appeared as if her whole countenance had become even more wondrous to behold.

Next up was the purple fairy. She walked up and

gave a slight curtsy to the king and queen before she gave her blessing. She placed her hands upon Rose's throat and said, "May your voice be pure, sweet, and strong. May it match the notes of the lark and the swallow and may you bring a lovely cadence upon the land!"

Just then the door blew open from an ominous outside force. A swirl of black and green blew inside and solidified before the king and queen. It was another fairy. She was not as beautiful and flawless as the other fairies. Her skin was a mottled black and grin and her wings were small and tattered.

"I wish to bestow a blessing upon my child!" she demanded. "Seems a shame that I was not invited." Her eyes bore into the queen's in accusation.

Louanna gasped as she realized who the fairy was. She grew pale white as the fairy came closer to them and grabbed Rose's hands. It was as though the king and queen were frozen in that moment and could not stop what was to come.

"My blessing is this, that on the evening of your sixteenth birthday you shall prick your finger on a spindle and fall into a deathly sleep. May you be known as a thorn unto all the land." An eerie green light flowed into Rose's hands and she let out a tiny cry of pain. The fairy leaned down and kissed the top of Rose's head and whispered, "May you sleep long and well, daughter." She then stood and disappeared within a green mist that dissipated. A loud croak could be heard as the fairy disappeared.

The king shook as if from a dream and turned questioning eyes at his wife. Louanna lowered her head in shame. This was not how things were supposed to go down. Tears fell freely from her cheeks as the room now grew ominously quiet.

"Ahem," someone coughed.

The king looked up to see an orange fairy looking at them intently. "What can you do?" he asked.

"I cannot undo her curse, but I can alter it," the fairy admitted. The king nodded, giving the fairy the go ahead to give her blessing.

She placed her hands upon Rose's heart and called out, "My blessing is this! That though you will sleep for a hundred years, you will then be woken by a true soul's kiss! May your heart shine true and may you bring healing unto all the land!" Her orange glow flowed into Rose's heart causing the girl to giggle. The orange fairy smiled at the little one as she pulled her hands back and moved away.

"Thank you!" The queen exclaimed.

"It was the least I can do, my queen. I only pray that it is enough."

The fairies bowed their heads as they turned and left the palace one by one and disappeared. The room was still very quiet and the royal couple did not feel much like celebrating, however, they knew they had to break out of this funk one way or another.

"My fellow subjects! Let not our hearts grow troubled! This is a day of celebration! Let's celebrate!" The King shouted. He was met with loud cheers and encouragement. They would celebrate for he had a beautiful daughter and she had a fighting chance.

*****

Rose twirled about the castle, singing gaily as she went about. Her heart was full of wonder and excitement. Everywhere she went there flowed a wave of peace and contentment over the land. The kingdom had never witnessed such peace in a very long time. The joy that came with it as Princess Rose went about was a sweet solace to the realm. Within those years, everyone had come to forget the curse that had been placed upon her. Rose never knew of the curse, for it was forbidden to tell her by threat of death.

The beautiful princess had cause to be extra excited this day. It was her sixteenth birthday, and all the preparations were being made. She would be crowned princess as was custom, and all the kingdom would rejoice with her. Her long golden hair flowed freely as she continued to twirl and dance and sing. Occasionally, she would grab hands with a passerby, whether it be a cook or a maid or someone else, and would twirl and dance with them. Rose was known for making everyone feel special, no matter what their station.

Rose was making her way towards the kitchen for a bite to eat when suddenly she spotted something small out of the corner of her eye. She stopped to take a better look at what it was that had gone by her when she spotted a bright green frog sitting on a bench and watching her with its big blue eyes. Something about those eyes were familiar to her.

"Hello, tiny frog. What are you doing here?" Rose greeted him with a smile.

The frog let out a loud croak as it hopped off the bench and then hopped a foot away from her. It turned its head to look at her with a beckoning glance.

"Oh, you wish for me to follow you?" Rose asked curiously. The frog croaked in reply as it hopped another foot.

Rose followed the frog as it continued to hop towards one of the large castle towers. She had not really gone this way before and was even more curious now as to why the frog was leading her there. She followed the tiny thing to the tower door, where it stopped and waited for her. She stood next to the frog and reached for the door handle. Finding it unlocked she opened the door and allowed the frog to enter first.

It hopped over to a flight of stairs that led up to the very top of the tower. Rose followed the frog as it continued up the stairs. It was a long winding stairway that curved around the tower itself. Rose was careful to stay close to the wall the farther up she went. She did not want to become victim to such a treacherous fall. Her heart beat faster the higher she climbed. She had never been this high before, and it was frightening.

Finally, they reached the very top and came upon another door. Rose looked down to implore of the frog, but he was gone. She looked all around her, but the frog was nowhere to be seen. He had simply vanished. Not knowing quite what to do next she decided to open the door and see what was inside. As she opened the door she was met with a strange green glow. This intrigued the girl more, so she entered the room to discover what was inside. An old woman sat next to a wheel that had wool attached to it. She was making the wheel spin and turning the thread into yarn.

"Come in, dearie. Do shut the door behind you. It gets awfully drafty up here," the old lady said kindly.

"Oh, of course," Rose complied. "Mother crone, what is it that you are doing there? I have never seen such a contraption."

"This? Why this is called a spindle. It is a wonderful tool to help spin my wool into yarn. How have you not seen one? They are quite common." The old woman raised a bushy brow as she asked.

"I am not sure, to tell the truth. It is fascinating," Rose said quietly.

"Would you like to give it a try? A beautiful young girl like you ought to know how to use it," the kind old lady offered.

Rose was elated at such an offer. Her smile lit up the room and seemed to dim the green glow slightly. The old lady took her time getting up from the small stool that sat next to the spindle and moved over so that Rose could take a seat. Rose sat gingerly upon the stool and looked at the contraption scratching her head. The old lady made it look easy, but Rose had no clue what to do.

"Mother crone, what do I do?" She asked.

"Oh, forgive me dear. I'm so used to using it that I didn't think that you would not know how," the old woman sighed. "First thing you must do is touch the needle to make sure it is sharp. You always want a sharp needle in order to spin your wool properly."

"Won't it prick me? Seems like it would be painful," Rose asked cautiously.

"If it is sharp then yes, but that is a good thing dearie. It will sting just a tad bit, but the pain won't last. Now, go on then, give it a try," the old lady encouraged strongly.

"Alright, if that is what one must do then I suppose I should," Rose submitted. She reached out her slender hand and touched the tip of the needle, just as the old lady had advised. The slight prick to her finger made her jerk her hand back as she let out a little shriek. "Ouch! That really hurt!"

Rose examined her finger to make sure it was alright. Little beads of red blood formed on the tip of her finger. Rose sat and stared at the blood in fascination. The old lady watched quietly behind her. Suddenly the room started to spin, and Rose started feeling sick.

"I'm not feeling so good. I feel faint," Rose whimpered before she fell from the stool with a thud onto the straw strewn floor.

"I dare say you don't, dearie. It has begun," the old lady rumbled with a deep masculine voice. She transformed into a tall man with long black hair and deep blue eyes. His skin had a bright green tint to it, giving him a sickly look. "I have waited a long time to exact my revenge. May your kingdom suffer greatly! The king took the love of my life so now I take the love of his!" He vanished amid a greenish glow. The green glow dissipated after his departure, leaving the still form of Rose behind.

*****

The queen was walking along the corridors as she headed towards the throne room. Louanna felt a sudden prick in her heart and had to stop to catch her breath.

"Something is wrong! Guards!" Louanna shouted. They came to her side within minutes. "Go, find Rose! I need to know that she is okay."

They left immediately to do as she bid, calling others to join in the search. Louanna took a steady breath and continued to the throne room. She needed her husband more than anything right now. Only he could bring her the comfort she needed.

As she entered the throne room she froze. The king was sitting ramrod straight on his throne with a man standing before him. The look on her husband's face was of sheer horror. She turned from looking at him and focused on the man standing there. He was dressed in a purple wizard's robe and held a long staff with a glowing green orb on top of it. His long black hair flowed down to his lower back and his skin was tinted bright green.

"Hello, Louanna," the man greeted huskily. "You are still as beautiful as ever. Even after all these years."

"Thaddeus Thorn, to what do we owe the pleasure?" Louanna sneered.

Now that she realized who the guest was, she tilted her chin up high, gathered her skirts, and walked proudly to her throne by her husband's side. She grabbed the King's hand for reassurance as she looked warily into the wizard's eyes. Something about those eyes seemed oddly familiar to her and it had not dawned on her until now.

"And there it is! The wheels are turning in that uptight brain of yours. The fair maiden who chose to be a queen rather than spend her days by my side. A man who loved her with all of his heart," Thaddeus bowed mockingly.

"What have you done to Rose?" Louanna barked.

"Oh, have you forgotten so easily? Sixteen years does make one forget," he whistled as he winked at her.

"No! It can't be!" The king shouted. "We destroyed all spindles and forbade anyone to make or use them. There is not even one in all of the kingdom!"

"Tsk tsk. Did you not think I could conjure one up with the snap of my fingers? It was so easy!" Thaddeus taunted.

"Thaddeus, how could you? She's your

daughter," The queen cried out too late. The king turned to his beloved bride with a worried and confused look upon his face.

"Louanna, my love, I don't understand," he begged. She could not look him in the eye as shame took over and tears fell from her lashes.

"I'm so sorry, Rowan," she whispered.

"Aw, poor King Rowan Briar. She didn't tell you about the deal she made, did she? No, I suppose not. Such betrayal," Thaddeus stated dramatically.

"Shut it! You have no right to talk to me in that way!" King Rowan demanded. He turned to the woman he loved with imploring eyes.

Louanna breathed in deeply before telling her tale. "It was many years ago, when I was but a young maiden and the world was full of wonders. I met a mysterious man on my sixteenth birthday. His name was Thaddeus Thorn. The very man that stands before you today. He was charming and alluring. I fell for him instantly. He wooed me and I just knew he was the one for me. Then, I celebrated my birthday with the kingdom and my parents placed the royal crown upon my head. I was now a crowned princess and it was my duty to abide by our laws. Those laws included an arranged marriage between me and Prince Rowan of the Briar Kingdom. I met the prince that night. He was tall, regal, and quite handsome. He too was charming and treated me well. I thought to myself, was it possible to love two men at the same time? Even if it was it didn't matter. I had to make a choice. Do I leave my kingdom forever and be with the mysterious man who stole my heart? Or do I do what is right by my kingdom and choose to be with the man that I knew I could love just as equally?"

"And... what did you choose, all wise queen?" Thaddeus mocked. Her eyes bore into him like darts.

"I chose to do what is right by my kingdom and be with the man I grew madly in love with! What you do not know, oh mighty wizard, is that I had not originally made that choice." She waited for that to sink in.

"What?" Thaddeus asked with a raised brow. The king listened quietly and patiently.

"I had chosen you. I packed up a bag of clothes that very night, grabbed some money and jewels to help me get by, and went off in search of you. I found you, Thaddeus. Do you know where?" Louanna demanded.

"I wouldn't know. I don't recall seeing you that night," he replied, completely dumbfounded.

"I found you deep in the woods. I don't know what you were attempting to do there but what I saw was enough to make my skin crawl and run the other way," she sneered. All the color drained from Thaddeus face. "Yes, that's right. I found you standing there in that eerie green light of yours. You were reading from a book of incantations. I could feel the darkness emanating off of you as you read those evil words out loud. A young animal lay slaughtered upon some alter that I assume you made. As I said, I do not know what your intentions were, but I knew then that I could not spend my life with a man who practiced in the dark arts." Louanna sat erect in her chair, posed like the queen that she was, and with no fear in her eyes.

"You could have had it all, Louanna. Much more than ruling a kingdom could ever have gotten you!" Thaddeus spat. Louanna ignored him and turned to the king.

"My dearest husband. Please forgive me for keeping this truth from you. I thought that I could leave this part of my past behind forever. Now, I see the error of my ways. Can you ever forgive me?" Louanna asked.

King Rowan gave a cursory glance towards Thaddeus and then looked into the eyes of his wife. "Louanna, I can forgive any and all of your past. That is an easy thing to do. What I am still a bit confused about is why you said Rose was his daughter. I fear to ask it of you, but have you broken your vow to me, my queen?" The sadness in his eyes tore Louanna's heart in two.

"I was tricked, my king. I don't expect you to believe me in this, but I do hope you will. When I was barren and my heart could take it no more, I cried out and begged for a chance to provide you with an heir. It happened then that a tiny frog popped out of the fountain where I poured out my woes and told me he could make a way for me to have a child with you. I was desperate and willing to do whatever it took. That is why when we next consummated, I mixed your semen with the frogs. It was what the frog had said needed to be done. I thought nothing odd of it at the time, though now I see how dark and evil it truly was. Still, we had our daughter after that." The tears flowed freely and she had to stop to wipe her eyes. "It occurred to me after that our daughter might wind up being ugly and repulsive. I could not bear the thought. So, I went to the fairies and besought them. I begged them to give specific blessings upon our child so that she might be the beautiful young woman she is today. When I saw the dark fairy and how she cursed our child, I was beside myself with fear. It was only by the grace of that last fairy that we know our daughter will live. Forgive me, I beg of you."

The king remained silent for some time as he contemplated the astounding tale his wife had told. He had no reason to not believe her, but all of it still perplexed him. He looked up at the wizard and paid more attention to the man as he stood there brooding. "So, this is the frog then? You had no idea?", he asked.

"No, my king. I had not a clue," she whispered sincerely. He gave her hand a gentle squeeze.

"Thaddeus Thorn, you are an evil wizard. Tell me, who is Rose Briar's father?" the king asked calmly. It amazed Louanna at how calm he remained through all of this.

"She is both of ours. Our semen was fused with magic. Your blood and mine flow through her veins." Thaddeus stated sourly.

"I see. So tell me this then, why would you curse your child to die?" A flare of anger surged in the king's eyes.

"It was the ultimate sacrifice and perfect

revenge all wrapped up in a neat little package," Thaddeus hissed.

"What are your intentions now?" the king demanded.

"To watch your kingdom fall and continue to see Louanna's heart break," he gloated.

"Then you have failed," the king declared.

"How so?" Thaddeus asked as he stood more erect.

"Our daughter lives! And you do not know the queen the way I do! She is strong, compassionate, and pure of heart. I forgive her completely and I will always be true to her and the kingdom. Now, I command you to leave this kingdom! You are hereby banished and are never to return on threat of death!" The king's voice bellowed and echoed through the throne room.

"How dare you threaten me!" Thaddeus shouted. He took his staff and aimed it towards the king.

"Fairies!" The king cried out.

Instantly six fairies stood in front of the king and queen, facing Thaddeus. Each of them had a menacing look upon their faces as they aimed their wands at him. He knew that he was no match for all of them at once and vanished in a swirl of green smoke. The fairies lowered their wands, turned to the king and queen, and bowed before them before dissipating in thin air.

"Do you truly mean it, Rowan?" Louanna asked. Her sad eyes begged for him to forgive and accept.

"Yes, my love. And in a hundred years I will prove it to you," he held her hand to his mouth and lay a kiss upon it before they both fell into a deep slumber.

Meanwhile, a soldier had found Rose lying on the floor of the tower. He commanded a few of his comrades to bring up a royal bed for them to lay the princess upon. He placed the bed in the empty room near a window and lay the sleeping princess gently upon it. Then he had soldiers lined up and down the stairs to guard the tower. Two soldiers stood outside the tower as well. Then the leader, who it was that had all of this set up, closed the door behind him and stood just outside it with another soldier before all the kingdom fell into a deep sleep. These were the orders given by King Rowan of the Briar, should they find the princess fast asleep and unable to wake.

To be continued...

'Til Death
Kayla Krantz.

What will you do when love drives you to madness? After falling for Rapunzel, all the prince can dream about is rescuing her. When he sees his opportunity to take action, he sees his dream turn into a nightmare.

Love was not something the Prince had ever
believed in. So when he first saw her, he thought he
would be ill for his own ignorance, his own lack of
capability to understand the greater forces beyond
life. He had seen his father go through it with his
mother, and countless knights and servants
resigning to follow their own passions, but he had
never experienced the lure for himself. Surely no
one could be perfect enough to invade his every
sense, and yet, someone had.

Every way he could think, this girl was there
dancing in the shadows of his mind and forcing him
to question his own foolishness. Every day, when he
first woke up, he thought of the fateful day his
world had changed. Sometimes, he tried to tell
himself it had all been a dream, but he knew better.
Even fleeting thoughts of her made him smile for
his own dumb luck.

*****

Her voice had been the first part of her that had alerted him to her existence. Her singing, like a siren's, had filled his ears and made him feel as if he was floating. Never before had he heard something so beautiful and that thought brought him to madness, filled him with desperation to see what kind of goddess could create music like that, sounds capable of changing his entire belief system in an instant. It seemed impossible, and yet, here he was just the same. With the madness seeping into his blood, he needed answers. It couldn't be a human woman capable of such sorcery.

It had to be a witch.

But in all the stories he had heard, witches were ugly, despicable creatures who harmed children and fed off the pain they caused. Had he ever heard the story of a witch who sung dulcet tunes? He couldn't remember. The easiest way to know would be to see for himself. If it was a witch on the other side of the music, well, he'd cross that bridge when he came to it.

Pushing through the trees, he stumbled out into a clearing and froze, stunned into an immobilized stance. The tower that stood before him was enormous, shooting upward into the sky so that the top was hidden in the clouds. For all the Prince's travels through the woods, he had never seen this building before; never known that anyone could call this place their home. How long had it been here without him noticing?

The mast of the tower was composed of solid bricks and grey chunks of concrete pressed together round and round, broken only by a long line of golden paint. The prince blinked and paused. It wasn't paint, it was hair—a long golden silver rope that glowed like the purest of diamonds in the pink light of the rising sun. Delirium pushed the madness deeper into his brain and he was desperate to get into the tower, to get to the bottom of this mystery. He was so determined to achieve his new goal, that he could hardly remember his life before hearing the woman's voice.

All that mattered was seeing her.

He approached the tower, fingers brushing the dirt from the stones before he looked up, at the strands of golden hair tickling his nose. It was so long, and the distance so impossibly dangerous, that he had a moment of clarity and questioned himself. Was this really the best move he could make? As soon as the thought appeared, it vanished. With shaking fingers, he reached up to grasp the hair, gently at first, and stroked a piece with his thumb. When his skin came into contact with the soft rope, his impulse control was lost. He grabbed it, wrapping the delicate strands around his hand like it really was the mere length of rope that it resembled.

At first, he tugged gently, looking up desperately for the sound of pain or cries of outrage. The singing continued without a pause, and the Prince was even more confused. He stared at the beautiful hair wrapped snugly around his hand and the bricks in the tower wall and looked up, gauging the height of the tower. If he made it a considerable distance, the fall would kill him. That much he knew.

But he was brave, wasn't he?

He had to be. He was a Prince, after all.

So, he began to climb. Minute after minute, he tried to control his breathing, only looking upward at the trip he had left rather than looking down to the progress he had made. If he made it, he would thank every god in the sky. At first, he was sick with adrenaline, but when he reached the halfway point, he was sick with anxiety and anticipation. Fingers shaking, he touched the cold stone of the windowsill and paused, uncertain of his next step. What would she do when she saw him?

What would he do when he saw her? Suddenly, he felt foolish. What was he doing? Where was his sense of strategy...of logic? Then the singing stopped, and the Prince held his breath. He broke his own rule and looked down, at the green grass yards below him. He grabbed the window ledge tighter, convinced he would fall.

He didn't.

"Hello?" A sweet, tiny voice floated out from the inside of the tower.

A shadow blocked out the sun and the Prince looked up...and then he saw her—the most beautiful maiden he had ever laid his eyes on. Her green eyes stretched wide and her pretty pink lips puckered into a perfect 'O' when their eyes met. When he saw the pure concern—no trace of malice, confusion, or fear—he knew she was the One. He had never been more certain of anything in his life.

That first meeting in the woods was usually the first thing the Prince thought of when he woke up. That first glimpse he had gotten of his Princess would be forever burned into the back of his mind, he was sure. For a girl who had been secluded in a tower for a majority of her life, she was not shy.

While she was reserved, she had showed him all the manners of a proper maiden of the castle and he was impressed. Her personality, matched with her beauty, was a deadly combination—something the human mind could hardly comprehend, let alone forget. And even thinking of her fleetingly caused a giant smile to break out across his face. How could he be so lucky as to have her in his life?

He stared at his reflection in the bathroom mirror and watched as the smile drooped on his face, the sunny thoughts in his head turning sour as the complications of his new reality reared their ugly head. If she was a normal girl, she could've—and would've—been moved to the castle where she would be pampered and properly cared for.

That couldn't happen in this situation…or at least it couldn't happen without some real work being put in.

"Father! Father!" the Prince had panted as he burst into the King's private chambers upon arriving home that night.

Wide-eyed at the intrusion, the King turned, furious and the anger only slightly subsided when he realized it was his son behind it. "Spit it out, child," he said with a dismissive wave of his hand.

Red in the face and panting for breath, the Prince paused, and hunched over to put his hands on his thighs, and forced his words through his teeth. "There's a Princess in the forest!"

The King's bushy eyebrow raised skyward. "A Princess, you say?"

"Yes, Father. Where is Bryn?"

"You will not drag my Knight Lieutenant out on one of your ridiculous quests," the King said, chin raised. "If it's the heart of a lady you require, you must earn it yourself."

"At least let me borrow a Squire. Please, she's in trouble. She's in this tower and—"

The King's eyes went wide, and he took a step forward. "She's in a tower?"

The Prince bobbed his head so fiercely that it hurt.

"You must never return there," the King said in a voice that sounded both confident and afraid.

The Prince was confused by it. "But—"

"No buts!" The King roared and jabbed his jeweled scepter into the floor with a heavy thud that made the Prince wince despite experiencing similar scenes to this for a majority of his life. "That is an evil place, watched by evil forces."

All the Prince could think of was the gentle girl in the tower. Anyone who was cold enough to lock her away like she was nothing but a rabid animal was definitely an evil he couldn't fathom. "That's why I need to save her, Father."

"The Enchantress' business is no concern of mine," the King said and turned away, briskly giving his son the cold shoulder. Literally.

"The Enchantress?" the Prince tried to ask but the King was no longer listening. He strolled through the chambers, exiting through the door on the opposite side of the room before slamming it loud enough behind him to ensure the Prince that the conversation was over, and he was truly alone in his quest.

The Prince spent that night trying to conjure up images of the evil woman in his mind, but nothing seemed to fit. Thoughts of ugly witches were all that came to mind and with it, the feeling of danger seemed dim and dull. When he had met his Princess, he had charged in without fear not knowing if she was a witch or not, so why be afraid of one now?

The next day, the Prince visited his Princess again, this time with a load of questions he needed answers for. She was so happy to see him, smiling wide enough to show all her perfect teeth and wrapped him in a hug with all the strength her tiny body could muster. Then he had asked who the Enchantress was and the warmth left the girl's body. She was cold, stepping back and biting her lip.

It was fear on her face. That much he was sure of.

"What has she done to you?" The Prince had asked.

The girl had only shaken her head, staring off distantly into the corner of the room instead of making eye contact. She wouldn't answer his questions, and suddenly, he felt bad for even bringing the subject up.

As time went on, the Prince began to wonder if the Enchantress had just been his father's way of trying to keep him from going into the forest for whatever reason. Sure his girl was afraid of the mention of the name, but he never saw hide nor hair of her. Days turned to weeks which turned into months, and he grew closer to the girl in the tower, fearing the Enchantress would make an appearance, and yet she never did. Every time he walked into the clearing, it was with a lump in his stomach, convinced that she would be there waiting to hex him into oblivion for discovering her secret.

But she never was.

The Prince had considered asking his girl—Rapunzel—about the Enchantress but when he was around her, it was easy to believe that evil did not exist outside of his mind. Surely if this girl had been exposed to such witchcraft, she would show it. Other than the time he had brought up the Enchantress directly, Rapunzel was always oozing happiness, and shining with a radiance that was so bright it was contagious.

So, the Prince kept visiting the beautiful princess and his confidence rose day by day. When he went home, back to his cold lonely bed at night, he let his mind wander to the 'what ifs.' What if she was here? What if she lived a normal life? What if she was his bride? Then, the territory became dangerous. What if he could free her from the tower? How could he free her?

Any real Prince would've rescued her on that first day,

The Prince scrunched his face, hating that voice, but also unable to ignore the fact it was right. I'll rescue her today, he shot back at it as if it would respond.

It did not and he turned away from the mirror to get ready for his day. He didn't know how he would pull her from the tower since her hair was the only way in and out that he could see, but he was determined. A feeling in his gut told him that today would be different from the previous ones.

He would save her or die trying. That was a promise he would swear by.

Bravery had been the Prince's greatest trait and flaw. It dragged him into situations before he was sure he could handle them—as proven by his initial meeting with Rapunzel—but in the same breath, it overwhelmed him. When he thought there was something he should do, he obsessed over it until it was done.

Thinking of his Princess alone in that cold tower made him sick. She seemed happy but was she really? Or was it only because she didn't know any different?

After eating the dinner Rapunzel had made, the two held each other in her parlor room, staring out of the window and into the thunderstorm beyond. They were quiet and content in each other's company. The Prince dared a glance at her, into her eyes, and wished he knew exactly what she was thinking.

"What's it like...outside?" She had asked, voice so quiet he hardly heard her over the rain.

The Prince had been unsure how to answer.

Rapunzel had misinterpreted his silence and murmured, "Maybe I'm better off not knowing," before breaking away and going to her bathroom.

The Prince hadn't known what to make of that reaction, but he felt worse for it. Did she have any faith he would rescue her? Or did she not want to leave the tower? That thought had never occurred to him. Could it be that she didn't consider herself to be a prisoner? That was depressing and left him wondering even more—did she even want to be his bride? He wouldn't let himself believe she didn't. In his mind, it was so easy to see the way her green eyes lit up each time he hauled himself over the windowsill, the way she squeezed him tight when he pulled her in for a hug. He loved her, and she loved him too.

So why had he never asked her if she wanted to be free?

The Prince pushed the thought to the back of his mind. Of course she wanted to be free. It was why her hair always draped from the tower. It was the one part of her that could escape the tower, and she seized that opportunity every day. She wanted to be rescued, wanted to find a way to explore the world outside of the tiny slice of life she was forced to live; and today would be the day he gave her that, gave her everything she wanted and needed, and they would start their happily ever after.

He trudged out of the castle, glancing over his

shoulder to see who would take notice of his movements and considered trying to find recruitment like he had wanted to do on that first day. He remembered his Father's words again and stopped the search, holding his chin high as he left the castle grounds. This was his mission and his alone. Foolish as it might be, he wanted to prove to Rapunzel just how brave he could be.

The walk through the woods seemed quicker with the determination pumping through his blood and when he emerged into the clearing, he looked up at the sky, watching as the last few rays of the day's sun bled away into the darkness. Then, his eyes were on the tower, on the shimmer of moonlight on her beautiful hair, and he hurried forward. He had never visited her at night before and his heart pounded at the thought. What would she think of it?

Her hair is down. She must've expected me, he reasoned as he began to climb.

In the shadows, the climb was easier. He couldn't see the distance to the ground and the not knowing made it easier to keep his nerves calm. Even with the excitement pressing on his chest, laboring his breathing, he didn't have a care in the world as he climbed. All he could think about was holding his precious princess in his arms again.

A day was a long time to go when one was in love.

When he reached the top, he reached up for the window ledge, fingers scratching at the cheaply painted wood, and hauled himself from the rope of hair. The second his feet landed on the floor, he was aware of how wrong the entire situation was. He couldn't see his Princess. It was darker than the night outside in the little room. The moonlight streaming in provided the only light and he paused, the hairs on the back of his neck standing on end as he glanced over his shoulder, out into the open window. The Prince had never seen it this dark. When he turned back toward the room, he couldn't even see his own hand when he waved it in front of his face.

"Rapunzel?" he asked, already knowing he wouldn't receive an answer.

On an ordinary day, Rapunzel would've wrapped her arms around him the moment his feet landed on the floor. The silence was just as unlike her as the darkness. The Prince tried to push away his unease, waving his hand through the shadows with the faint hope that she was playing with him and would spring from the shadows at any moment in an attempt to scare him. His hands moved through empty air. She wasn't here and yet…he turned back toward the window again, studying the strands of silver gold hair.

Then he froze.

His sweetheart's hair had been nailed to the wall beside the window, connected by a thin pink skin dripping crimson down the wall. A small puddle had accumulated on the windowsill, just out of reach of the spot his hands touched when he climbed across. Upon seeing it, the heavy smell of iron filled his lungs, and he could hardly believe he had been able to overlook the sight and the smell for as long as he had.

He retched instantly, bending over to accumulate the action, but the contents of his stomach did not come up. Through watery eyes, he looked up at the scalp, watching in horror as the nail suddenly came loose, splattering through the blood, and the hair rushed away through the darkness outside. The Prince dove forward but the delicate strands were long gone before he even came close. Eyes bulging, he swallowed out of despair and studied the window frame before taking a step forward to peer outside, at the castle around the window, and then the wall just inside the room. There was no other way out beside the rope of hair he had climbed to come in.

The only opportunity to escape was gone.

"True love lasts forever!" a wicked voice called from the ground, the person responsible invisible in the inky night.

The chill down his spine was enough for him to be sure it was the Enchantress. She knew about him, so she had known what he had with Rapunzel too. She knows everything, a voice whispered sickly-sweet in his ear.

His heart skipped a beat.

"Rapunzel!" he shrieked and whipped around to face the dark room once again, fearful of what the shadows might contain.

He didn't expect a response and didn't receive one. Heart pounding, the Prince knew he would have to do something but had no clue what that should be. As he stared into the inky blackness of the unknown, all he could do was chastise himself. How could he have ever considered himself to be brave? A brave man would've charged through the danger, the unknown, and found their girl without a thought for their own safety.

Then there was him—a man who stood staring into the room as if something would suddenly appear and give him all the answers or protect his girl from the danger he could not. The Prince looked toward the window again, knowing that his only true escape was gone, and saw the blood again. Rapunzel's blood. The first tear leaked down his cheek at that thought and his body switched to autopilot as he moved forward, zero confidence in his body or mind.

Rapunzel's living space consisted of two parts—the parlor room with the tiny kitchen and bathroom—and then there was the bedroom. He had already come to the conclusion that she wasn't in the parlor room. Whatever the Enchantress had done, she had left his beloved in the bedroom.

"Rapunzel?" he called again, desperate to break the silence the only way he could.

The house was so cold without the sound of her voice to warm it.

As he traveled through the room, his mind could only see the chunk of her scalp, and against himself, he tried to picture what condition the Enchantress had left his love in. If she was still alive, she would no doubt be in agony. He fought down the urge to vomit as he sought out a candle. Two steps forward, before his hands had a moment of opportunity to blindly search through Rapunzel's things, a light illuminated the room, halting the Prince's progress as he lifted his hands to shield his eyes.

Blinking rapidly, his eyesight adjusted, and he realized how tidy, how empty, Rapunzel's house looked. Where she had had stuffed animals and figurines, there was just cold empty air, minimalist furniture, and that sickening feeling of anticipation washed through him again. If the Enchantress was behind this, then she wanted him to see. If he was right, what layed on the other side of the door was most likely something he did not want to see.

He stayed in the middle of the room, overtaken by the intensity of the moment. The last thing he wanted to do was walk through that door, but how could he choose otherwise? What if Rapunzel was still alive and he could save her? He would never forgive himself if he tried to escape now without seeing what had become of her.

"I'm brave," he tried to tell himself, but the words lost their meaning. The past ten minutes had already proved he had never been brave in his life and he was sick of pretending. He was a coward, selfish, and concerned only with himself.

Even though he could see, he set his hands to the wall as he moved to brace himself, not fully trusting his jelly-like legs to hold him steady. There was something comforting about the familiarity of the wall, something comforting about the memories it brought. The Enchantress could empty every belonging out of the room, but the walls would

110

remain, whispering fragments of memory to him to give him the strength he couldn't conjure on his own.

Then he was in front of the door and all the memories in the world could not drag him away from what he was sure the next minute of his life would bring. When his fingers brushed the knob, he couldn't bring himself to move through the tremors that wracked his body. How dare you call yourself the King's son? he chastised. You can't even open a door. Some Prince.

He pulled in a breath through his teeth and as he let it out, he twisted the knob, the hinges creaked louder than he was used to as the door slowly opened. The light from behind him spilled into the space occupied by the darkness, a silhouette of his form breaking it up.

"Rapunzel?" he managed to cry out, much to his own surprise. His throat was so swollen from his silent sobbing that the one word hurt to say, and he couldn't imagine ever speaking again.

Taking in a breath, he stepped over the threshold and a flash of light spread through the room, causing him to pause once again. This time, however, he held his eyes closed a second longer than was necessary, knowing he would be forever changed when they opened again. When he finally let them flutter open, his heart descended to his stomach and bile pooled at the base of his throat, just enough to taunt him with the idea of vomiting without making it happen.

The bedroom was neat and immaculate, the way

Rapunzel had always kept it. At first, the Prince had thought she was tidy because she was bored but he had come to realize that it was her personality. Cleanliness gave her a sense of control in a situation in which she had none. It was admirable in a way.

The Prince kept that thought in his mind as his eyes swept over the familiar layout. In one corner of the room was a vanity table attached to a mirror, always empty of all cosmetic products except for her overly used hairbrush. On the opposite wall lie a white dresser. In between these two pieces of furniture was the corner that housed her 4-poster bed draped in royal purple sheets and blankets. By themselves, they seemed so normal—a scene he had witnessed a dozen times during his visits with his favorite girl.

The Prince was struck by the normalcy and looked upward, his entire world crashing down around him.

There was his beloved Rapunzel, a thick lock of her own beautiful golden hair wrapped around her torso, all the way up her upper body to hold her arms above her head before finally ending in the knot tied to the rafters in the ceiling high above. Her white nightgown was red with blood. Her head was down, and the Prince could see the white of her skull through the blood and chunks of fresh skin clinging to her scalp. Her face was angled toward the floor—one small blessing—whatever emotion had haunted Rapunzel in the final moments of life was most likely still written on her features.

And that was one image he never wanted to see.

"Rapunzel," the heart-broken sob tumbled from his lips as he sank to his knees. That was when he noticed the writing on the wall behind the bed, massive letters running in some places, enough to deform the delicate lettering.

'Til death do you part, it read.

His eyes dropped to her bed and in the corner, he noticed the twisted portion of Rapunzel's sheets. A voice in his head screamed for him to turn around and leave the room, to count his losses, and try to find a way out of the tower, but his body disobeyed him. He took one step closer and the smell alone made him wish he had stayed by the door. Fingers shaking, he grasped just the edge of her silk sheet to peer at what was wrapped inside.

It was a lump of red-purple tissue, oozing blood in some places and congealing the same substance in others. He paused. It wasn't tissue. It was a heart. Her heart, slashed, abused, and dead. This time, the Prince did hurl, all over his shoes and the immaculately clean floor of Rapunzel's room. His vision swam and before he knew it, he was falling to the floor, his head thumping against the floorboards a moment before he blacked out.

*****

When he came back to consciousness, it was still dark and the smell of his vomit less than an inch from his face filled his nose and made him feel as if he was about to throw up a second time, except there was nothing left in his stomach to lose. He sat up slowly, his vision still black around the edges, and was horrified to see that Rapunzel's body was gone.

The heart, and the message, however, were still there. For a moment, he wondered if it he had imagined what he saw except when he closed his eyes, he could picture the horrific white gleam of Rapunzel's skull and knew he wasn't capable of imagining something so horrible.

The Prince shot to his feet, through the door and out into the parlor room, determined to catch the Enchantress if she came anywhere near him.

"Show yourself!" He snapped out to the darkness beyond the tower.

No response.

Helpless, the rage melted away to despair and an ugly sob rattled through his chest. He looked around, breathing wildly as he lifted his hands to shove his fingers through his hair. What would he do? What could he do? He was trapped, alone, in a tower in the middle of the woods.

Who would even know he was here?

Father will know, he assured himself but that brought little comfort. His father had warned him away from this place, told him it was a bad idea, and the Prince had made his decision. Father won't come. It was a cold thought but true nonetheless. The Enchantress, the Prince thought and another sob fell from his lips. Somehow, someway, she had known that tonight he was going to take Rapunzel away from her forever and done what she could to stop him.

But how did she know?

And what did that mean for him? Would she leave him here to starve? Or would he be tortured like his precious Rapunzel had been? He closed his eyes as her name drifted through his thoughts. His precious beautiful Rapunzel was gone, and he couldn't summon a single vision of her to his brain that didn't revolve around the moment of her death. All he could see was the binds of her hair, the blood on her nightgown, the remains of her heart.

That witch is going to pay, he decided, clenching his hands into fists.

The temporary shot of anger fueled him to do a lap around the parlor room, searching for anything that could be used to get him out of his situation, whether it be to climb down the tower or wait for the Enchantress to make an entrance and fight her on his own terms.

You don't know if she'll even come back, that voice reminded him.

And just like that, the anger was gone again.

What better way to punish him than to leave him up here in the tower to either starve to death or eventually leap to his death? The Enchantress would never have to set foot here again, and she would win. The Prince slowly slid down to the floor, that thought at the forefront of his mind.

He could understand now why the King had been so upset at the idea of the girl in the tower—he must've had a brush with the Enchantress at some point in his life, something that would teach him to never interfere in her matters. The Prince could only wonder what story his father had never bothered to tell him.

I should've brought help, the Prince thought and rested his head against the wall, staring up at the ceiling. Should've, could've, would've. He had doomed himself. Aren't I supposed to be the savior in this story? No. He knew the answer now. He was more helpless than the Princess he had been determined to rescue. Before he had come along, she had been alive. Lonely but alive, nonetheless.

What kind of hero gets the one thing he loves killed?

I need to get out of here.

If he didn't, he would drown in his own despair. What a pitiful way to go. With an eye twitch, he wondered if the Enchantress could read minds or feed on energy. The last thing he would do would be to entertain that monster.

Shakily, he rose to his feet, pressing his fingers to the wall again. He could get out of the tower if he tried hard enough. There were always answers. Slowly, he approached the window again, ready to gauge the distance from the window to the ground below. He paused when he realized Rapunzel's beautiful golden hair was back, tacked to the wall by the thin bloody flap of skin.

The Prince paused, tilting his head to the side in confused consideration. It had fallen upon his arrival, hadn't it? The Enchantress had taken it, he was sure. Carefully, he stepped forward, fingers, touching the closest piece of hair. It was real. Convinced he was still delusional, he grabbed a handful and yet it remained.

Heart pounding with a mix of excitement, adrenaline, and relief, he glanced over his shoulder, to the blackness of the room behind him, and began to climb. As he descended through the darkness, all he thought of was making it home, to his bed. He would mourn the loss of his dear Rapunzel then he would exact his vengeance against the Enchantress for taking her away from him.

Freedom, he thought, drawing in the cool night air to wash the scent of blood and vomit from his nose.

Just as his feet touched the grass at the base of the tower, he closed his eyes to revel in the victory and when they opened, he was once again an inch from his own vomit on the floor in Rapunzel's room.

It was a dream, he realized and fresh despair washed over him as he lost his freedom all over again.

Slowly, his eyes looked up and he saw her— Rapunzel still swinging from the rafters and he closed his eyes, losing himself into a mess of tears on the floor.

*****

When he cried himself hoarse, he wandered from the bedroom, unable to stay close to his beloved's corpse for another moment longer. He expected to see sunlight filtering in through the window in the parlor room, but it was still black beyond the open square. The Prince took in a shuddering breath and instantly went to the window. The hair and the scalp were gone, their only evidence of them ever existing was the smear of blood on the wallpaper still evident even in the shadows.

The Prince glanced over the wooden edge, into the darkness of the shadows outside the tower. In the back of his head came the images from his dream, the anticipation of his freedom. The cruelty of having it ripped away made him briefly consider jumping out of the window just to beat the Enchantress at her own game.

But that was the game, to some degree, wasn't it?

Even though the hair rope was gone, he was determined to not give up. He would find a different escape, even if it took all he had to do it. After all, anything was possible if he wanted it hard enough. With a deep breath to steady himself, he darted back into Rapunzel's room, gathering any and all blankets and bedding he could find before dumping them into a large pile on the parlor floor. He shifted it then went to the bathroom and tore down the shower curtain, gathering it into a bundle with all the towels he could find. Satisfied he had gotten them all, he threw them onto the floor with the blanket pile and sat down beside the mess.

Quickly, but with steady determination, he began to knot the various fabrics together. What felt like hours later, he had a rope made of towels and blankets. He pulled them, making sure the connections were secure, before he tossed one end over the rafters. When it came back down, he pulled on both ends, testing the strength of the cloth rope, and was pleased to see it held his weight.

Satisfied, he tugged it free and when the end fell back into his arms, he bundled it together, praying to a God he wasn't sure would hear him, before he moved over to the window. With the same emotion that helped him thread together his rope, he pried the bloody nail out of the wall, tears stinging his eyes as he caught sight of the blood on the wallpaper again. Trying to push the thought to the back of his mind, he speared the nail through the end of his rope and pounded it in place with the side of his fist. He tugged hard on the rope, testing the nail, and it held.

The Prince lifted a hand to ruffle his hair and studied what he was doing—the rope, the nail, and the drop that would kill him if the invention failed. He had to try it though, didn't he? What other choice did he have?

With that thought as his motivation, he tossed the rope over the edge of the windowsill and into the black abyss of night. The nail still held, and the Prince studied it before looking back over his shoulder again. He didn't feel good about it. The creeping sensation of déjà vu washed over him, but he ignored it as he stepped over the wooden windowsill and placed himself in the best position to begin his climb.

The second he put his full weight on the rope, he expected something to go wrong—the rope to fall apart or the nail to inch out of the wall—but they did not. He put one hand over another and grew gradually closer to the ground, inch by careful inch. When he reached the halfway point, the Prince dared to allow himself the hope that the would make it. Perhaps this time would be the time to get away. Heart thudding in excitement, he closed in on the last few feet and jumped to the ground, relishing in the feeling of something solid under him after being suspended in mid-air for so long.

He closed his eyes to breathe in the smell of the grass and when his eyes fluttered open, he found himself back on the floor by Rapunzel's bed.

*****

The Prince screamed out, a mix of pain, confusion, and frustration. Now he knew he hadn't been dreaming. He had made it out…and somehow the Enchantress had put him right back in the tower. Perhaps he had never left at all. Maybe it was all in his head, a carefully constructed illusion by the Enchantress to torture him in more ways than he gave her credit for.

Carefully, he sat up, fearful of seeing Rapunzel's body once again, but thankfully, it was gone. He tried to not put too much thought into that—what her disappearing body could possibly mean—and stood on legs that shook with uncertainty but were also solid with sadness. His first thought was to build the cloth rope again, but when he studied the windowsill in the parlor room, he saw that the nail was gone.

If he was to escape again, he needed a new

plan—something he hadn't tried yet. He wondered if it was worth the effort to come up with a new plan. If he made it out of the tower again, wouldn't the Enchantress just put him right back in the same spot? Maybe she would do it again and again until he went mad with desperation.

Perhaps she was trying to kill him with a broken heart, the metaphorical death to the literal one she had inflicted on his love.

That's insane, he tried to tell himself. There has to be an explanation, but I can't focus on that. I need to get out. I need to get help.

He chanted that thought so many times in his head that it began to lose all meaning.

So, the Prince looked around, trying to scour up any plan he could manage. There were sharp things in the kitchen, knives and forks, but would any of them be strong enough to wedge in the mortar between the bricks of the tower wall? The Prince got up and moved to the kitchen, trying not to think of how much Rapunzel had loved to cook as he pulled out every knife he could find, stabbing them into his skin to test the sharpness.

As he had suspected, they were dull, but he wouldn't let that stop him. He wouldn't let the Enchantress win so easily. He rifled through all the drawers in the kitchen and eventually found what he was looking for—a sharpening stone. It seemed too good to be true, but at the same time, it wasn't out of the ordinary to find something of the sort in the kitchen of a woman who spent a good majority of her time cooking.

The Prince took the stone and sharpened everything he could find, once again testing their sharpness on his own skin. After he was finished, his hand wept with the blood of a hundred different cuts and punctures, but he hardly felt the pain. He was confident in his new plan. He found a roll of duct tape in the counter by the trashcan and went to work taping the sharpest of the knives to his knees. Then, when he was finished, he stared at the silver tape and the shiny blades.

He looked ridiculous, he could see that, but did it matter if the planned worked? Could it work or was he just so desperate to win that he had lost all sense of reality? It scared him that he couldn't answer that question so instead, he wandered aimlessly to the window and looked into the abyss. The cold air rushed around his head and he thought about what it would be like to just leap from the window, through the air, and end it all. Would he die instantly? Or would he be in pain.

Rapunzel was in pain, the voice whispered.

The Prince had to clamp his eyes shut to hold in the tears. Focus, he said, opening his eyes. Through the watery haze, he looked up, at the shining full moon far above his head. As beautiful as it was, it only served to make him feel worse. It should've been daylight, if the amount of time that he felt had passed was real, but time had frozen on the exact moment the Prince's feet had touched down in Rapunzel's tower. The Enchantress had somehow put him in some type of time warp where he was forced to relive the same hour over and over.

Evil bitch, he cursed in his head as he stepped up onto the wooden windowsill and let his legs dangle into nothingness. Then he had the thought— she could've made Rapunzel relive the moment of her death over and over, and suddenly, the Prince knew that things could always be worse.

As half of his body hung over the ledge, the feeling of open air made his heart pound. Any issue he had from this point onward would cost him his life. He knew that but also had the mild curiosity of what would happen if he did die. Would he wake up in the same spot on Rapunzel's floor again or did the game end when his heart did?

The Prince wasn't sure, and would be perfectly happy never knowing the answer to that question if it meant he could go back to his own life as if none of this had ever happened.

Angling himself awkwardly, the Prince jabbed the first knife into the wall, pleased that it took much less force to sink it in then he imagined it would. He took in a breath, knowing the next moment would literally be life or death, and swung off the window ledge, trusting the knife to hold him long enough to sink the other one into the wall. He stayed put. Breathing roughly, he told himself not to look down, but then did so anyway and swallowed roughly, too petrified to move. The wind breezed through his hair, tempting him with thoughts of freedom, and very carefully, he unwedged the knife on his left hand from the wall and began to make his way downward.

Each jostling movement terrified him,

convincing him that he was about to slip and lose the game at any moment, but he made progress. By the time he was halfway down the tower, his hands were bleeding from the force of the handles jabbing into his skin and he was sure his knees were in similar shape, but he didn't stop, he wouldn't. His confidence was building and as he approached a safe distance to the ground, he wanted to scream out his delight.

When his feet touched into the grass, he paused, almost expecting to open his eyes and be back in Rapunzel's room, but when he opened his eyes, he was still there, at the base of the tower.

Tears of joy bubbling in the corners of his eyes, he hurried to rip the tape off his knees, letting those blades fall into the grass, though he didn't discard the knives he had kept in his hands. Keeping one in each hand, he bolted into the trees, not caring that he could hardly see where he was going, he was just glad to be free.

If the Enchantress was waiting, he would find her and end things once in for all.

Then, his luck changed.

Running full speed, he ran into a tree, blinding pain searing from the point of impact in his forehead, all the way down his abdomen and radiating out toward his back and neck. He crumpled to the ground, staring up at the dark leafy branches far above, and closed his eyes, trying to get the pain to disappear.

When he opened his eyes, the pain was gone, but he stared at Rapunzel's purple duvet once again.

*****

This time, he didn't care about the smell of his own vomit or the congealing blood of Rapunzel's heart. He stayed on the floor and cried until his face was raw and his throat burned. Never before had he felt such sadness in his life, and now, he couldn't imagine feeling anything but. It overwhelmed him, stealing every ounce of energy and motivation he had left. He was perfectly willing to spend the rest of his life right there as long as he never had to move a muscle. He cried until no more tears would come. Then, violent sobs racked his body, and when even those tapered into silence, he stared up at the ceiling, feeling as if he was caught between this world and the next.

The situation was clear to him. There would be no leaving the tower, just as it had been for Rapunzel. I took her place, he thought solemnly, and thought back to that conversation with Rapunzel, the first time he had mentioned the Enchantress to her. She had been so afraid.

Now I know why, the Prince thought solemnly, understanding everything with sudden clarity.

How was it possible to feel dead and still be alive?

Gasping for breath to fill his aching lungs, he rolled onto his back and let his eyes drift to the ceiling. With a jolt, he realized Rapunzel was back, her body once again hanging lifelessly from the rafters. The Prince would've started crying all over again if he could, and was almost thankful that his fit had numbed him to the point that emotions were beyond him. In some strange way, the sight of her back with him, comforted him.

There was a way they could still be together. Who says love has to end with death? Love lasts forever, the Prince thought and wiped his face.

He breathed in, trying again to regain himself against the exhaustion caused by his crying fit, and realized the scent of decay was heavy in the air. When he studied Rapunzel's skin, it no longer looked ample and newly dead, it was sagging and looked dry. With horrified realization, he knew she was rotting. The Prince held his eyes shut, unable to comprehend this. Decomposition took a good bit of time, but time didn't seem to be moving in his little slice of Hell. Had he really been locked in the tower that long or was Rapunzel's appearance another trick of the Enchantress'?

I have to get out of here, the usual thought rung out inside of the Prince's head. Though he was more reluctant to answer it this time than he had been in his previous experiences.

On feet that felt more like rocks than part of his body, he walked out to the dark parlor room, to the windowsill, studying it for any signs of the hair rope. It was gone again but the nail was back. The Prince was unsure what that was a sign of at this point, but he reached up to ruffle his hair, thinking of what plan he could try this time. The cloth rope hadn't gotten him very far. As soon as he reached freedom, it had been ripped away. The climbing devices made from the knives had been more successful or enough to get him to the woods at least.

In his mind, his attempts were all failures, no matter how far he had gotten. He was still here, still trapped, and out of ideas of how to escape. So, what could he try now? Briefly, he thought of trying to create the climbing devices again, but a quick survey of the kitchen showed that the knives and forks were gone.

So much for that, the thought pounded at his temples and he realized a migraine was beginning to form. He almost laughed at the sensation. It was something new at least. Maybe it's my brain bleeding from the curse, he thought and began to laugh until he cried again. What a terrible place he had to be at emotionally to wish that thought was true. He sank to the floor with his back to the wall and buried his face in his hands until the ugly wretched sobbing stopped again. His face was so raw it stung to the touch, and his throat was thoroughly tight.

Dead inside, he stood to his feet again, shuffling his way into Rapunzel's room. Even with the horrible smells assaulting his senses, it felt less lonely with her nearby. The Prince stood on the threshold, staring at Rapunzel's body, and studied the way she hung so carefully from the rafters. In that moment, all he let himself feel was the love he had for her and approached with small, shuffling footsteps. With barely any ounce of awareness, he stepped closer to the rotting corpse. The smell was worse the closer he got, but he didn't let it stop him.

He just wanted to be close to her again, to feel the warmth and the love that had drawn him to his own damnation.

He set his hand on her soft sheets and pulled himself up on the bed. Tears still on his face, he approached Rapunzel's swinging body on his knees and stared at her bloody gown an inch from his face before he wrapped his arms around her lower waist. In his head, she was alive, and they were spending just another day together. He could hear her laughter, her singing, and with the fresh wave of pain in his heart, it was easy to ignore the horrible rotting smell of her skin and the stickiness of her bloody gown.

"I'm so sorry, Rapunzel," he cried again, squeezing her so tight that a bit of cold blood leaked down onto him.

That would've broken him if he hadn't already been destroyed. When the cold liquid touched the bare skin between his shoulder and neck, he looked up, out of habit. He could see her face then, the one part of her he promised he wouldn't see. Her face was ashen gray and her emerald green eyes were covered over in a white film. He hardly recognized her and the longer he stayed there, gazing up at the rotting mess his beautiful to-be bride had become, his thoughts turned to wonder.

Rapunzel had been tied to the rafters by a lock of her own hair.

I can use it, the Prince thought, studying the way the golden tendrils dug into her skin from the effort of suspending her in the air.

Breathing in deep, he braced himself, tucking his fingers under the tightest part of the knot around her stomach. Rapunzel's skin wasn't as dry as it had appeared. Pressing into it through the gown left him with the impression that his fingers would slip through an opening in her flesh and into her organs. He stopped at the sensation, turning away to vomit once again.

"I can't do this," he said out loud, staring into Rapunzel's dead eyes.

This was the worst choice of his life, and he wished the Enchantress would've killed him right from the start. Like the coward you are.

The anger flared, but didn't ignite anything beyond that. He was still dead inside, still faced with this impossible choice, and still utterly, utterly alone. So he stepped back from the situation again and surveyed his options. The more he looked, the more amazed he was that he actually still had choices he could make.

Untying the rope from Rapunzel's body would take a lot of contact that he wanted to avoid at all costs. He eyed Rapunzel's regal dresser and grabbed it, hauling it over to the space between the bedframe and the vanity mirror before he climbed on top.

The distance to the rafters was still high above his reach, but when he stacked the vanity chair on top of the dresser, he could stretch just enough to touch the knot. With tender fingers, he untied her beautiful hair from the beam and slumped onto the bed, face down. The Prince was almost grateful for that. Looking into her dead eyes just once had been too much to bear.

Slowly, he climbed down and looked at his beloved's body sprawled out on the bed. Now that she had moved, the hair rope had inched out of place, leaving only bloody marks where it had been embedded in her skin. The smell of decay was even stronger now, and he gagged, but thankfully, did not vomit again.

He studied the length of hair but knew that without the portion that had been tied around Rapunzel, it wasn't long enough to even reach halfway down the tower. If he wanted to make this a real effort, he would have to get all of it, even the part soaked in his dead love's blood. With shaking fingers, he touched the hair around her stomach and felt the bile pool in his mouth. The golden strands were sticky, reeking of body fluids and old blood. The chill of the fluids stung him.

It was hard to believe Rapunzel had ever been warm, ever been alive. Biting his lip to gain composure over himself, the Prince tried to hurry and unknot the tightest bind of the harness. The more he tried, the more of the old blood he smeared over his fingers. The longer the moment dragged on with no results, the more frustrated and despaired he became.

When he was ready to call it quits, curl up next to Rapunzel, and wait to die, the knot finally came loose. He prayed and let out a silent "thank you" as he tugged on the strands, pulling free only a bit of it. To get the rest of it loose, he would have to turn

Rapunzel over.

The Prince closed his eyes for a long moment. Of course, he thought because this was the Enchantress punishing him. What better way than by making him cradle the corpse of the one person he had loved more than anything in the world? It was cruel, it was unjust, it was despicable.

It was also his life now, so he did it, both disgusted and heartbroken by the act. This would be the last time he'd ever hold her after all, the last time her tiny body would be cradled in his arms, and the more those thoughts overtook his brain, the harder it was for him to put her back onto the bed once his mission was successful.

If this really did work, and he was free this time, did it really even matter? Rapunzel had been his life's purpose and the thought of going the rest of his time without her made it seem so empty, so impersonal, so cold, but he didn't know what else to do but to fight for his survival. After all, the human body craves to stay alive for as long as it can.

Even when the brain is unsure of the reason why.

The Prince set her down and gathered her bloody hair, the last part of her he would ever touch, and left the room. There was no need to look back over his shoulder at her, he would see her forever. In the crevices of every dream, nightmare, and instance of blackness of his life, she would be there. He moved onward, into the dark parlor room, and just like in his very first attempt, he looped the hair into the nail in the window frame and tied it tight.

Sobbing, and wishing for a death he was no longer sure he could achieve, he began the climb down, no longer relieved for the feeling of the free air or the thought of the grass beneath his feet. He was numb to it all. So numb in fact that when he touched down, closed his eyes, and once again woke up in Rapunzel's eyes, he did nothing but lie on the floor.

*****

This time, he was resolved, resigned to his fate. He knew what he had to do if he truly wanted to get out of the tower. If he really wanted to wake up in a place other than this, to never lay eyes on his dead love again, he could do that. Just not in the way he had originally hoped.

Though now the option seemed like a blessing if he ever knew one. The faintest hint of a smile touched his lips as he rose to his feet. He took no notice of his vomit, of Rapunzel's heart, of Rapunzel herself. None of it mattered anymore. One careful step after the other, he walked into the darkness of the parlor room, sure it was the final time he would see it, and once again filled with a sense of gratitude for that thought.

He would not miss it. Any of it.

Then his eyes zeroed in on the window frame and the hint of a smile transformed to a full-on grin. He walked toward it and climbed onto the wooden windowsill. It was nice to not worry about a plan, to not care about what tomorrow would bring. As far as he could tell, he would never experience tomorrow anyway, and even if he did, it wouldn't be worth the pain. So, he sat there, staring up at the cold light of the moon and feeling the crisp night air blowing through his hair and across the exposed skin on his neck and hands.

The slight chill broke out gooseflesh across his arms, and he rubbed it away, the ridiculous crooked smile still on his face. Then, his eyes went from looking up to looking down. It was blackness below him, and he let himself fall from the ledge, never feeling freer in his entire life.

Secret Swine

Victoria Taylor

"You may know well the tale of the Three Little Pigs, but what you do not know is that this is not the true story. Rather, it is a much diluted and mixed up tale that got spread around and lost in translation. Allow me to share with you what really happened."

I know you have heard the tale of the Three Little Pigs. Three brothers who all set out to make homes for themselves, but could not agree on what they wanted it to be made out of? The first one chooses straw, the second one chooses wood, and the third one chooses brick. Then there is this supposed big bad wolf who would hunt them down to eat them. He succeeds in blowing down a couple of houses, but the pigs get away and wind up holed up in the brick house with their brother. Yada yada yada... and so on, right? He huffs and puffs but can't get the house to fall. So, he gets this bright idea to go down the chimney like he's ole' Saint Nick or something. The pigs get smart and build a fire to cook him up and that's the end.

You ever stop to ask why the pigs would cook up the wolf? Why is it that the wolf was so keen to go after these pigs when there was plenty of other game out in the woods to go after? No, not little red, that's a whole 'other' story. And why do they go and make the pigs seem so smart, innocent, and brave while the wolf is made to look like a dumbass? Does anyone ever question these things? Or do you just take the tale for what it says and tell yourself it's just a little myth told to keep kids in line then move on? Well, I'm going to tell you a very different tale. One that may well get me dead, but let's face it, the truth needs to be told and I am the most likely candidate to tell it to you. I'm going to tell you how it all really went down. There were not just three little pigs. Oh no! There were also three big pigs. That's right! And this is how the story really goes...

*****

Pluck, Tuck, and Curly stood in the tall mansion's wide hall, waiting to be received by their elder brothers, Hunk, Flank, and Rig. They had just come back from a wild hunt, and were there to report and check in. If Rig had his way, he would make sure they were out on another hunt very soon. There was no rest for these little piggies. They shivered as they waited. It was evident that they feared the older ones.

"You don't think Hunk will throw us in a pit again, do you?" Curly whimpered.

"Better than being thrown on a spit and turned over a fire with an apple in your mouth," spat Pluck. Tuck remained somber and silent as they continued to wait.

"Don't say that, Pluck! It could happen!" Curly cowered.

"We didn't come back empty handed you nit

wit. We got one of them. It's just a matter of luring him after us somehow," Pluck admonished.

"How are we going to manage it? It's not easy to lure one of them," Tuck spoke up quietly.

"I'm thinking. I need more time!" Pluck growled.

"Time is not on our side, brother," Curly moaned. Just then the doors opened to the grand living quarters of their elder brothers. The servant bowed and beckoned they enter. They did so with much trepidation.

Pluck led the way in as the others followed with tails tucked between their legs. Their elders sat rigidly in high backed chairs that resembled thrones and waited for the little ones to stand before them.

"What news do you have for us?" Rig demanded. The pigs stood stock still before them all trying desperately to not piddle themselves where they stood. They three were your average pink pig with various blemishes to show the differences between them. Their elders were much larger wild boars with tusks that could strike a deadly blow with one hit, and large bristles that could well do some damage themselves. The youngers knew not to anger their mighty elders and would strive to not do so at any cost.

"My lord, we have lured one. We but need some more time to ensnare him. I assure you it can be done," Pluck spoke up quickly.

"How much time?" Flank demanded. "I hunger and long for that sweet savory sustenance that is endued with magic. I can never get enough of it!" A line of drool fell from his mouth and lingered a moment before dripping onto the floor. All three elders were salivating now, just at the mere thought of eating the magical flesh.

"Give us a week, sire. I assure you that flesh is yours." Pluck grew emboldened as a plan began to form.

"Very well, you have a week. No more than that. Should you fail, it will be your flesh on the spits!" Flank laughed hoarsely. The other elders joined in his maniacal laughter, causing the little pigs to tremble in fear. They were dismissed by the flick of a hand and quickly bowed out of the room. As soon as they left the mansion they started talking fast and all at once.

"What do we do?" Curly asked.

"Do you really have a plan, Pluck?" Tuck asked.

"We need to build a trap!" Pluck exclaimed. The other two looked at him with wide eyes.

"What sort of trap would actually work?" Tuck asked fearfully.

"One that does not look like a trap," Pluck snorted.

"Really, Pluck, this is no time for games. Our very lives are at stake here," Curly reprimanded.

"No games dear brothers. We shall build a house. An enticing house. One that will gain the attention of our prey," he explained.

"And we are the bait as usual, aren't we?" Curly pouted.

"Do you know of any one else who would qualify?" Pluck laughed. Curly and Tuck punched him lightly in the arm. He feigned pain, but it was all in good fun.

They walked on for some time in silence as they pondered what kind of house it should be that they would make. What would entice their prey to come after them?

"I say we go with a straw house. We lure him in, then set the whole thing ablaze. Easy Peasy," Curly suggested.

"No, a straw house would burn up too quickly, giving our prey time to escape. I say we build a wood house. Lacquer it with just the right substance to keep it burning once it's lit," Tuck suggested.

"You both are thinking too small here. Our prey will want a challenge. I say we build it of brick. Lure him in and then use the house as an oven!" Pluck suggested.

"You think we are so small and dumb!" Curly yelled, clearly hurt by his brother's words.

"Curly is right, you always lord over us like we are not your equals. It's not fair," Tuck whined.

"What are you two going on about? I've always been the leader of our trio. Why is now different?" Pluck demanded.

"It just is!" Curly and Tuck cried out in unison. They argued over it for a while until Pluck grew weary of their complaints.

"Fine! We will each build our homes and see which one succeeds. Deal?" he offered. The other two agreed. They would each pick a spot in the woods, a fair distance from each other, and see who would succeed in luring the prey and capturing it.

"Who knows, maybe we will each succeed and have three of them to take to the elders!" Pluck encouraged. The brothers merely frowned at him and soon all three were off to build their little homes that were to be the hidden snares that would lure the prey to them. If all went well, one of them would succeed and bring the elders the flesh they so longed for. Should they fail, well they just did not want to think of that option.

*****

So, what do you think so far? Do you see where this tale is going? I've gained your attention at least, right? Those three-little pink piggies had three big burly mean and ugly brothers who lorded over them and forced them to do their bidding. It is the truth of it. I swear it to you. I have no reason to lie about any of this. Still, I suppose you will need to know more if you are to believe me. Very well, I shall continue the tale. Pay close attention now...

*****

Curly stood before his straw hut and admired it. It had taken him a good long day to get it all built and fixed up and he was very proud of his handy work. It was dusk now, and that meant that he needed to be ready. His prey would soon be onto him. Sure enough, he heard the not so distant howls as the sound of leaves began to rustle.

"Who...who's there?" Curly called out. A figure

came from out of the shadows, standing tall and proud before him.

"Hey there, little pig. Won't you let me come in?" The voice was gravelly, but not harsh.

"Not sure I should, not even by my hair on my chin," Curly replied as he lifted his nose to the air.

"Come now, it's cold out here and I could use the company."

"Well, I suppose I could allow you to warm yourself by my fire. Though I would think a wolf would not be so cold with all his fur," Curly grimaced.

"In my natural wolf state yes, but not when I'm in this phase. I need warmth to get me through until the next full moon. Would you be so kind?"

"Oh, very well then. Come inside," Curly offered.

"Thank you," the wolf-man said as he walked inside the straw hut.

Curly rubbed his hands together with glee. He had his prey exactly where he wanted him. As the man sat by his little fire to warm himself, Curly shut and locked the door. He then walked over to the fire and sat in the chair across from the wolf to study him and decide how best to capture him.

"Would you like a blanket?" Curly asked, his words dripping with kindness.

"It would be most appreciated, thank you. My name is Felnir, and I am indebted to you, my friend." Felnir bowed his head.

"Tis' nothing. I would not want to be left out in the cold myself. Do to others as they say and whatnot," Curly blabbered.

"Yes, so it is said," Felnir laughed as he wrapped himself up in the blanket.

Curly saw his chance as he watched the wolf-man cover himself. He stood quickly and made it appear as if he were merely stoking the fire. As Felnir closed his eyes Curly took the prod and caused a hot coal to leap onto the blanket. It caught fire instantly.

"Oh my!" Curly cried out as he stood and watched the blanket burn. Felnir jumped up with a howl and began to huff and puff until he had enough air to blow the fire out. He managed to put the fire out on the blanket, but another spark had caught the straw of the house on fire and soon the whole place was burning. Curly saw that his opportunity had been foiled and with great trepidation, he fled the house and headed straight to his brother Pluck's wood house.

Felnir had managed to get the fire out but it was too late. The straw house had burnt to the ground. He stood a moment to contemplate and felt horrible about the little pig's home. He needed to apologize to the poor thing, and find a way to somehow make it up to him. He sniffed the air to catch the pig's trail, and was soon heading in Curly's direction. It took him little time to come upon the nice wood house that had a cozy warm fire pushing smoke out the chimney. He walked up to the house and knocked, but no one answered. He could hear whispering inside, and knew that someone was in there at least. He knocked again, only louder. It came out a bit harsher than he had intended, but he hoped that it at least got their attention.

"Little pig, please let me in. I want to apologize for your straw house. I really did try to save it, but it was too late. I wish to somehow make up for what happened," Felnir shouted through the wooden door.

"I am not so sure I should let you in, surely not even by the hair of my chin," Curly cried out.

"Come Curly, the poor wolf has apologized. Perhaps we should let him come in from the cold?" Pluck insisted.

"Oh fine, let him in then," Curly whined.

Pluck opened the door and smiled politely to the wolf. Felnir could tell that they were brothers, and was grateful for the second chance that they offered.

"Do come in and warm yourself by the fire," Pluck offered.

Felnir walked over to the fire with caution. He did not want a repeat of what happened back at the straw house. Still, the warmth of it beckoned him to come close. He sat down in a nicer more comfortable chair than the last one, and soon drifted off to sleep.

"Look at him all curled up like a pup in that chair," Pluck sneered.

"He looks good enough to eat doesn't he brother?" Curly snickered. Both kept their voices low as they discussed their plans.

"I will stoke the fire and make it bigger. The higher flames will catch fire to the wood and soon cook him within. You stay by the door so that we can make our escape," Pluck whispered.

"Very well, brother," Curly agreed.

Curly tiptoed over to the front door while Pluck tiptoed to the fireplace. Pluck checked to make sure that Felnir was fast asleep before stoking the fire and piling on more wood. It got so hot that Pluck had to back away quickly. Felnir mumbled something about warmth, but did not wake. Pluck watched as tongues of fire flickered out over the fireplace and soon caught hold of the wood on the outside. Soon the entire house was glowing with hot flames.

"Go go go!" Pluck whispered wildly to Curly. Curly opened the door and they both ran outside. Once they felt they were at a safe distance they stopped and turned to watch the house burn with the wolf-man inside.

Felnir's coughing had woken him and as soon as he realized he was surrounded by smoke and fire he began to huff and puff to put the flames out. He could not believe his misfortune and that he had caused yet another fire. By now the pigs would definitely not help him. He managed to get the flames around the door out just enough to barge through it and make it out of the house. He huffed and puffed even harder but to no avail. The house had burned to ash.

Forlornly he turned to see if he could find the pigs nearby, but they were nowhere in sight. He simply had to make it all up to them. What could he possibly do though? He wasn't sure, but he had to at least try. He sniffed the air and caught their scent.

As he followed their trail, he came upon a brick house. This was by far the sturdiest of the three houses and it looked very inviting. There was no fire in the chimney of this one and oddly that made Felnir feel much better. With great determination he walked up to the door and gave it a good hearty knock.

"Who's there?" A familiar yet subtly different voice called out.

"It's Felnir. I've come to give my sincerest apologies. I don't know what misfortune has come over me to have set fire to two of your houses, but I will do whatever it takes to make it up to you. Could you find it in your hearts to forgive me, yet again? I need the warmth of your home," Felnir begged.

"I do not think that wise, not even by the hair of my chin. You have burned down my brother's houses and you dare ask I let you in?" Tuck chastised.

"Yes, I do so dare ask. I would not if it were not so dire a situation. I beg you, please," Felnir whimpered.

"No, I think it would not be such a good idea. What if you set my house ablaze as you have done my brothers?" Tuck demanded.

"Then I would huff, and I would puff until I could do so no more. I would give it my very best that is for sure," Felnir assured the pig.

"You huffed and you puffed on both straw house and wood. Yet you did not save them as you surely could," Tuck continued.

"Yes, sadly it is true. Yet, even more reason to make it up to you," Felnir admitted as he wondered why they fell into rhyme. Perhaps it was this pig's way. He shrugged and hoped that if he continued along, he would be allowed entrance.

"Nay, I shall not let you in. Not even by the hair of my and my brother's chins. You have caused enough damage," Tuck declared.

Felnir could hear them move away from the doorway. He understood all too well why they would not let him in. He turned with shoulders sagged to leave the home and started to walk back into the woods. Then the sky had darkened as the moon was blotted out and Felnir could feel the madness begin to creep up inside him. No one was safe when the madness took over. He had to get inside before it could claim him. The pigs could not understand, and now he had no choice but to make his way inside.

He turned and looked upon the brick house and then spotted the fireplace. It was not lit and so that meant he could go down the chimney and enter the house in that manner. It was a very rude thing to do but what choice did he have?

If he didn't go in there, then the madness would claim him and the pigs would all be doomed. Still, he did not want to be completely rude so he shouted as loudly as he could to the pigs inside,

"Little pigs! Little pigs! I have no choice but to come in. I am coming down your chimney so do not be alarmed. I must enter your home so none will be harmed!"

He climbed up onto the roof top and cringed when he heard the pigs let out silent squeals. He inched into the chimney and started to scoot his way down it. As he continued down, he smelled smoke and it started to get warm. Much to his dismay, the pigs had started a fire inside the fireplace. Perhaps they had not heard him after all. He had to think fast on what the best thing would be to do. Did he push himself back up out of the chimney? Or did he continue downward and brave the fire? Was it better to chance another fire? Or to allow the madness to claim him?

Felnir chose to brave the fire. The madness was by far worse. He fell quickly to get through and hoped that he could roll out before causing too much damage. Instead of a fire he fell into a pot of boiling liquid. The pain that shot through his entire body as he fell into the pot caused him to howl. He pushed himself up and out of the boiling pot causing him to land on the floor with a loud thump. The three pigs squealed in fear as they watched the wolf-man hop up off the floor like nothing had happened.

The liquid from the pot had put the fire out completely, much to Felnir's relief. He shook like a dog to rid his body of all the water from the pot. The water flung all over the room and even hit the pigs. Feeling better, Felnir looked up at the three frightened pigs.

"My sincerest apologies little pigs. I had no choice but to enter your home. Otherwise, the madness would claim me and none of you would be safe," Felnir explained.

"You stupid wolf!" Tuck cried out. "You dull-witted numskull! You just don't get it do you?"

"Tuck, calm yourself man," Curly whispered.

"No! I'm done. If this wolf is that stupid then we should have no problem offing him," Tuck declared.

"We need a plan though, brother," Pluck suggested.

"None of our plans have worked. We act now!" Tuck shouted.

Felnir watched the pigs with a cautious eye. He did not understand what they were going on about, but could see that something was not quite right. He wasn't sure exactly what to do so he decided to offer assurance.

"I am so sorry that I have caused you all strife. I will be gone by morning so that you may all continue. Once I have phased again, I can help you rebuild your homes and I will do my very best not to set fire to them or destroy them."

"Can you believe this nim-wit? He still doesn't get it!" Tuck laughed. "Listen, wolf-man, we are not going to let you go. We are going to kill you, and then bring you to our brothers to feast upon. I'm afraid you've had it wrong all along. You didn't start those fires. We did! Our homes were meant to burn with you in them!"

Felnir could hardly believe his ears. These three pigs were out to get him this entire time? How could that be? He looked at them with sharp angry eyes, "What is your problem? Why snare me in such a way?"

"Oh, well for some odd reason our big brothers find you wolf-men to be somewhat of a delicacy. They enjoy feasting upon your flesh. I wouldn't know what you taste like so cannot say for myself if you taste good or not, but we have been hunting your kind for some time now," Tuck blubbered proudly. "We've been quite successful at it for a very long time but then you wolves got clever and were no longer lured by our traps. And our brothers grew angry. We had to come up with a creative way to lure you in. And look, it worked!"

"You think it worked? I am not bound by silver rope or lying helpless in a fire. Seems it failed to me," Felnir roared.

"Tsk tsk... you really do not pay much attention, do you?" Tuck pouted.

Just then a silver net fell over Felnir, dropping him instantly to the ground and rendering him completely helpless. Pluck and Curly stood on each side of him and secured the net about his body, tying him up.

"My brothers will be most pleased that we did not cause your flesh any harm. They much prefer to do the harm themselves," Tuck sneered.

"You will regret this!" Felnir snarled.

"On the contrary, poor wolf. I will enjoy this!" Tuck bowed before the wolf then walked out of the room.

Curly and Pluck walked to the kitchen to grab a bite to eat. All this hard work made them extremely hungry. Felnir salivated with hunger as he watched them eat. They sat and chatted away as though nothing had happened. This was all a bit much for Felnir. He had to come up with a way to escape. Still, he knew that this was better than allowing the madness to claim him. He would bide his time until he could make his move.

*****

Oh, how the tables have turned! Am I right? You didn't know that Felnir was the victim, did you? Do you still feel bad for the little pigs? Or do you now have a fresh perspective of how things really went down? It's amazing how the tales change as the years go by. Soon the truth becomes so twisted and you have nothing left of what truly happened. I do not know if my accounting will ever make it out there, but I do hope that one day it will. I can't live with knowing that others may not know what really happened. Sigh...perhaps I am boring you with my prattle? Very well, here is what happened next...

*****

Felnir woke to daylight pouring in through the window. He must have fallen asleep there on the floor and the pigs into their beds. He counted it a small blessing as he watched the sun rise. He had survived the madness and would make it through another day. He heard rustling in the other rooms and then one by one the pigs came meandering in. Soon the tantalizing scents of eggs and bacon permeated the entire house, as well as fresh coffee.

It was an odd sight to Felnir as he watched these pigs eat bacon. Did they know? Or were they ignorant to the fact that they were eating their own kind? He dared not say a word as he watched them. His stomach betrayed him as it grumbled loudly and caught the attention of the three little pigs.

"Aw...is the poor wolf-man hungry? Perhaps we should feed it?" Tuck mocked.

"Actually, it would be wise to fatten him up a bit," Curly suggested. Tuck glared at him. "Look, Tuck. Our brothers will see him in this state and likely throw us in a dungeon cell. We need to fatten him up."

Tuck growled but motioned for Pluck to bring a plate of food and drink to Felnir. They pulled Felnir up into a sitting position which freed up his arms so he could at least eat. Then they placed the food and drink inside the net so that he was able to reach it.

Felnir did not hesitate as he delved into the eggs and bacon with glee then he emptied the cup of coffee. The meal was so satisfying that he let out a contented sigh. He soon learned that that was a grave mistake.

"Oh, so you like eating pig, do you? And you wonder why our kind eats you?" Tuck spat.

"Were you not just eating your own kind not minutes before me?" Felnir growled angrily.

"How dare you!" Tuck was ready to punch Felnir, but his brothers pulled him away and attempted to calm him.

"Tuck, I don't know what your problem is man,

but we need to be clear headed here. I'll go get the cart so we can carry him off to the palace," Curly suggested.

"Fine!" Tuck shouted before he ran outside, slamming the door behind him.

Pluck just shrugged at Curly as they went about getting Felnir ready to go on the cart. Then Curly went to grab the cart. It took some effort, but they finally got Felnir onto the cart and each put on a harness to help pull the cart along. Tuck came up from behind and soon took lead. They took a wide path into the forest that led directly to the palace.

"We haven't much time, Tuck. We have to get him to the palace by nightfall," Curly whispered. Felnir wondered if they knew he had excellent hearing.

"We will get there in time. We just can't make any stops along the way," Tuck grumbled.

The pigs continued on in gloomy silence as each brooded over their situation. Felnir caught a whiff of a familiar scent nearby and soon gained some hope. He let out a loud mournful howl as he called out to his mate. He knew that she would follow him and do whatever it took to save him. The pigs looked back at him and laughed.

"The poor thing is in mourning," Tuck fake pouted.

"Good thing this will all be over with soon," Curly smiled.

"Well, that is after all the torture and being cooked alive!" Pluck laughed evilly.

They were suddenly in a good mood as they

chatted easily among one another. Felnir wished he could tear them limb from limb for all the taunting and pain they had caused him. It was not worth it, however. He was not that kind of man. He wasn't so sure about his mate, however. They had been separated a while back and he did not know if she had succumbed to the madness or not. He would be safe, but these pigs would not be. Did he care? Certainly, they deserved whatever fate befell them.

They continued on for an hour or two when suddenly Pluck cried out, "Tuck! We need a break man. My feet can't take much more!"

The cart came to a instant halt as Tuck put his face in Plucks with such anger that it made Felnir cringe slightly.

"I said no stops!" Tuck spat.

"Tuck, we need at least to stop and eat. Thirty minutes, no more. Just enough to eat and rest our feet," Curly suggested softly.

"Fine! Thirty minutes, no more!" he growled before turning away and disappearing into the woods.

"What is with him?" Pluck asked timidly.

"I don't know. I've never seen him this irate before. Maybe he just wants this done and over with?" Curly asked.

"Maybe. I'll be glad when it's all done. I could do with a nice mud bath and some good ale," Pluck admitted.

"Oh! That does sound good!" Curly agreed.

They sat under a tree and brought out some rations to eat. Stale bread, cheese, and water was good enough for the time being. Curly hopped up and brought some over to Felnir without a word. Felnir ate his morsels slowly as he watched the pigs eat. These two did not seem as bad as their brother and he wondered if they would even have done the things they had if it were not for him. The thought made him wonder if perhaps these older brothers that the three pigs talked about were the reason, they did any of this. It sure seemed that way. Would they make different life choices if they could?

A piercing squeal of pain echoed throughout the forest causing Felnir to cover his sensitive hears. Pluck and Curly stood quickly and looked about them with much trepidation.

"That was Tuck. Should we go after him?" Curly asked Pluck.

"I... I don't know. It might not be wise. Besides, our big brothers made it very clear that if one of us gets taken down then the other two keep going. We should do as they say," Pluck suggested.

"You are right. Poor Tuck," Curly sniffed.

They packed up quickly then put the harnesses back on to pull the cart. They picked up the pace in hopes to get to the palace before nightfall. Visions of what could have befallen Tuck roamed in their minds and caused them to shiver in fear. Felnir looked around the forest with keen eyes. When he saw a flash of silver fur, he knew that salvation was at hand. Tuck would be so lucky if she did away with him quickly.

The silver streak flew out and landed on Pluck and Curly, causing them to fall and drop the cart.

They both scrambled to get out of their harnesses, but the silver blur swatted them both across the cheeks. They squealed in pain as fresh blood dripped off their cheeks. The silver blur became a solid object and they beheld a large silver she-wolf. Her fangs were bared, and a deep rumble came from her throat. She was not happy with them and they could see no way out as they remained tangled in their harnesses.

"You will unbind my mate at once!" she demanded in a gravelly voice.

"Okay," Curly whimpered.

The she-wolf swatted the harnesses with her sharp claws so they could take the silver net off her mate. They did not hesitate as they ran back and untied the bindings then threw the silver net off Felnir. As soon as Felnir felt the strength return to his body he jumped up and did a somersault over to his mate. She nuzzled up against his side and he relished in her affection. Her eyes sought Felnir's and she said, "Sleep" as she breathed into his face. He instantly fell to the ground into a deep sleep. She licked his cheek before turning to the two little pigs that now stood shaking.

She walked up to them and put her large muzzle in their faces which brought more fear upon them. Once she felt that they were sufficiently overcome with fear then she transformed before them into a beautiful silver haired woman. Her naked body glistened in the fast fading sun. She basked in its warmth for a moment before turning back to the pigs.

"You have done an evil deed. Why would you enslave my mate in such a way?" she demanded.

They merely sputtered incoherently. "Very well, you pathetic pigs, I will truss you up as I have done the other one and we will get to the bottom of this. I will know exactly what happened and then I will deal out punishment as I see fit. Someone will pay for this! Of that, you can be assured!"

She trussed up the pigs with hair from her head. The bindings were stronger than anything the pigs had ever known. She put them in the cart up close to the front so her mate could have plenty of room. Then she picked up her sleeping mate and lay him in the cart with the gentle ease of a loved one. Her eyes were silver marbles that bore into the pigs as they trembled in fear. She then made her way to the front and shouldered the cart. The pigs squealed loudly as she took off with the cart so fast that everything around them was a complete blur. Before they knew it their brother was seated next to them, trussed up in the same way. Not even the fear of their older brothers could compare to the fear they were experiencing now.

*****

And now here we are! You may wonder how it is that I know the entire tale? That's super easy. I got to hear it from every point of view. Well from the point of view of the three little pigs and Felnir, my mate. It didn't take much to get those piggies to squeal. And oh, how I enjoyed every minute of it. I put each on a spit over an open fire. The smell of their sizzling flesh was most appetizing. They told me everything up to the very last detail. My poor Felnir slept through the entire thing. He was not happy with me, but did he blame me? What they did to him was so wrong. I merely returned the favor.

They begged me with pleading eyes after they confessed it all. I made like I was going to set them free then stoked the fires higher and watched them cook. I left them sitting there with fresh apples in their mouths and waited. I wanted nothing more than to share this meal with my mate, but I had something planned. I could smell them before they arrived. Larger than life they came trotting in like they ruled the world. I told you that this may get me killed, but I would die gladly if it meant getting rid of these filthy swine.

"What is the meaning of this!" Flank demanded as he entered. I watched as they entered, and I waited. He was such a pompous fool. The other two were at his side without so much as a word.

When they spotted the skewered little pigs, they let out loud growls. I guess I expected something more than that reaction but oh well. Turns out they didn't care much for their brothers.

"Your turn!" I shouted as stood before them. I swear saliva dribbled down their chins as they looked down at me with their beady eyes. "What makes you want to eat my kind? There are much more delectable things to eat in this realm." I had hoped to reason with them despite the madness that claimed me.

"Your magic has kept us eternally youthful and indestructible. We shall feast upon you this night. Our brothers will make a nice treat as well. I was getting rather sick of them anyways," Flank admitted.

"You are evil swine! I will make sure that the truth gets told. You will not get away with this!" I declared as I ran off as quickly as I could. I realized then that I could not take them on. Not if they were imbued with the power of my people. There was just no way I could win. I grabbed up my sleeping mate and ran for the mountains. The sacred cave was the only place we could stay for now. I only hoped we would be welcomed there. In the distance I heard the pig shout,

"Run all you want wolf! We will find you and we will win! We shall see whose tale wins out in the end!"

Hearts Bladed, Souls Serrated

A twisted retelling of the fairytale
Twelve Dancing Princesses
M.L. Garza

Dedication
To my supportive husband who always wanted to
see a cenobite crossed with a fairytale princess.
Weirdo.

Hearts Bladed, Souls Serrated
Twelve princesses, three nights, one horrifying
secret.
Every night, the king's twelve daughters go missing
and, and every morning, they reappear with worn
dresses and shoes. At a loss, he issues a challenge to
every eligible man in the kingdom: discover the
princess's secret in three days time and become a
prince, fail and lose their head. So far, no one has
been able to succeed.
Barro is a soldier still seeking the thrill of a grand
adventure. Gifted with an enchanted cloak and more
courage than wisdom, he knows he stands the best
chance at success where every other has failed. So
long as he is careful not to underestimate his
opponents, he may yet learn what secrets haunt this
mysterious castle.

A secret once learned cannot be forgotten, and a man who believes himself a future prince must earn it. When he discovers what the princesses are truly up to every night, it will take more than luck and bravery to see him through to the end. And if he cannot convince one of the women to help him in his quest to rid the world of evil, there may be no power in the world that can save Barro.

It seemed impossible for a man to ever lose track of twelve daughters, and yet that was the rumor circulating throughout the nation. Twelve young women, from dusk till dawn, completely unaccounted for but for shoes worn down to the delicate silk interiors and dresses threadbare as though worn for years each and every night. Such a mystery was enough to vex any father of one unruly daughter.

The king of Morvena was beside himself with twelve.

At first, he offered titles and lands to the man who could discover the princess's secret. Then it was treasures, increasing in value with every failed attempt. Other nations were worth less than what His Majesty was offering for the knowledge of his daughters' secret.

That too resulted in nothing.

The last he could offer, the one last true thing of

value a king had to give, was the daughter of a man's choice. If they could discover where the girls went each evening to destroy their clothing so thoroughly without the knowledge of guards or servants, they would marry the princess of their choice and be named prince and future ruler to the kingdom of Morvena.

This great prize came with one great warning, however: should these new men fail to discover the secret after three days, they would never be seen again. Whether their fates were death or something much worse than that, no one ever knew.

All anyone knew was that once a man entered that cursed castle, they never left it again, and no prince was ever crowned.

It did not take long for all the brave men to run out. Only cowards and wise men remained, for those were the only ones who would never go near the castle of King Weyn and his strange children.

Thus it was strange that one day, a traveler arrived to the kingdom, looking for a way inside.

Barro owned nothing, but that he carried it with him wherever he went. His horse he had from the war, still lively and true and scared of no man or beast that crossed their path. That life was behind them both now, yet they were both ready for one last adventure.

Morvena seemed as good a place as any for one such adventure to be found.

Perhaps there was one last brave fool to be found in the world.

The cobbled road leading to the village outside

King Weyn's castle wound like a great scaled snake. It slithered back and forth through the forest, then through fields and farms. At last, the first buildings appeared, and the castle itself glimmered in the distance. The serpent's nest. Or the dragon's, with its endless supply of riches waiting for him.

All he had to do was track down a few silly girls. How hard could it be?

On the village's edge sat a group of tents and stands belonging to foreign traders that often wandered the land. Not always welcomed by the townsfolk, Barro always looked forward to seeing their colorful emblems gracing the side of a trader's hut. Their wares included any number of strange, exotic goods from spices to furs to weapons. Some, it was rumored, even carried talismans of protection and other magical items.

This group of traders, however, seemed to have run afoul of the locals. A common enough occurrence, but Barro was not in the mood for it.

"Come on, girl," he said, patting his horse on her sleek chestnut neck. "Time to make a nuisance of ourselves."

"My money isn't good enough for you, old man?" One of the villagers was shouting at a trader in a stall. He waved about a leather purse that seemed full of coins. "Who do you think you are?"

"You could offer me a hundred times that amount, and I would not do business with you," the trader snapped back. His voice was strong and steady despite his advanced age, and he showed no fear in the face of so many angry people against him. Behind him cowered a young woman, his daughter most likely.

"You stuck-up, dirty, son of a—"

"Hey!"

All eyes turned toward Barro as he slid off his horse and approached, an easy smile on his face to hopefully ward off the worst of the ire.

"Who are you, stranger?" The angry villager demanded.

"Just a wanderer passing through," Barro said. "What's all this about?"

"This old man has decided he's too good for our money," the villager explained, turning his head back to the defiant trader.

Societal norms dictated that Barro side with his own people against the foreigner; it somehow brought people together to form a mutual hatred of the strange and unknown. Unfortunately for societal norms, Barro had no use for that. These villagers were no more his people than any other, nor was the trader any less.

"Then it looks like," Barro said, "that he has nothing to sell you."

The villagers and trader all looked taken aback.

"What did you say, friend?" The villager asked, advancing on him now. The old trader was momentarily forgotten in his anger.

"I believe you heard me." Barro released his horse's reins and rested his hand upon the hilt of his sword, ready to draw it should the need arise. "You should move along now."

"I don't think we've seen you around here,

stranger." So quickly did the term of friend no longer pass between people, and all for a few wares?

"I'm just a soldier passing through. I don't mean any harm."

"Then you'd best be on your way, shouldn't you? This doesn't concern you."

"My job is to maintain order, is it not? I think this does concern me." Barro flicked his thumb against the handguard of his sword, pushing it forward an inch so they could see he meant business. He wanted to reach the castle but there was time yet.

At last the men got the message. There were more of them, but it was clear none were armed with anything that could match a sword. These villagers were prepared to take on a half-blind old man and his daughter, not a Morvenian soldier.

One by one they wandered off, muttering under their breath over the unfairness of it all. Barro did not release his sword until the last one rounded the corner of a building and left sight. Only then did he relax and turn his sights to the foreign victims still huddled behind their stall counter.

"Are you alright?" He asked. "They didn't hurt either of you, did they?"

The old man shook his head and nudged his daughter to go back inside the tent. She glanced once at Barro and ducked beneath the heavy cloth, disappearing from view.

He always had a weakness for dark-eyed beauties…

"Thank you," the man said in a thickly-accented rasp. "You didn't have to trouble yourself in our problems, but you did."

"If I didn't, eventually they'd become my problem anyway."

"Perhaps so, but I still owe you my thanks."

Barro shrugged and glanced about the stall. Nothing here looked all that rare or out of the ordinary. "What did he want anyway? It looked like he was offering a lot of coin for whatever artifact you had."

"He didn't want any old trinket of mine," the old man snorted. "He was going to take my daughter from me and use her like some common whore."

Barro scowled, but felt the justification harden his heart against the villagers. Nothing could warrant such treatment of a woman, native or foreign born. It was a good thing he'd arrived when he did to stop it.

"Here," the old man said, handing him a wrapped bundle of fabric. "Take this with you as a gift for what you did for me."

Barro took it and unfolded a portion to look. It was well-made but did not appear to be anything special. A cloak like any other. "Thank you, but I already have a—"

"This is no ordinary cloak." The man took the bundle from him and unwrapped it fully. Still, it seemed nothing more than something one might find in any shop or market.

"What is it then?" Barro asked. Perhaps the man

was mad. Perhaps he should leave too.

"A magic cloak. It conceals the wearer from view."

He is mad. This is what I get for putting myself into other people's business...

"I truly am thankful for the gift," Barro tried again, backing up toward his patiently waiting horse.

The man smiled at him and donned the cloak himself. It only took a moment, and if Barro hadn't kept his eyes firmly on him the whole time, he wouldn't have believed it. Yet as soon as he fixed the clasp at his neck, the foreigner disappeared completely. It was as though no one were in the stall at all.

"Do you believe me now?" Said the empty air in front of him.

"How is this possible?" Barro gasped.

"It's best not to ask these things, traveler." The old man took the cloak off and he reappeared. "Accept my gift for what it is, and may it bring you nothing but peace and good fortune."

Barro felt his heart and hopes lift in jubilation. Perhaps there was some greater power looking out for him. After all, with such a trouble life he'd led up to this point, he was surely due some divine intervention and now was as good a time as any.

"I do accept your gift," Barro said, this time taking the cloak with a grateful smile. "And I know it will serve me well. I seek my fortune at the castle."

"The castle?" The man asked with a frown.

"Surely not to take up the king's challenge."

"The very same." He was confident when he road into the village, but now his success was assured.

"I have heard about the men who try and no one has heard about what happens to them after they fail. It is a doomed venture, boy. A fool's errand."

"Then a fool I am, but I am still going. I will be a prince or I will be nothing." Barro motioned to the cloak held lovingly in his arms. "With this, how can I fail?"

"It is enchanted, yes, but it will not save you from whatever evil lies in that place. You helped me, now let me help you. If you wish for a bride, I will offer you my daughter for she will be a good and obedient wife. You are a kinder man than the ones who tried to buy her from me. If you wish for a kingdom, use that cloak to win yourself your own nation. But do not enter that castle."

He was wise and anyone half as such would surely have followed the advice. The beauty in the tent could not be any less lovely than the king's mysterious daughters, and he did not miss the way her gaze lingered on him as she retreated.

But the challenge was half the fun, and he never was a very smart man. Clever enough to earn the ire of all commanders assigned over him, but it was not the same.

"I cannot stop you," the old man sighed. "I see the look on your face."

"It is true," Barro admitted. "I will go no matter what you say."

"Very well, then I offer you one last piece of advice."

The soldier nodded, bidding him go on.

"Trust nothing and no one once you enter that castle, traveler," the old man said. "If you were wiser, you would have been less trusting of me as well."

"And why is that?"

The old man peered up at him with his one remaining eye and just smiled. The other eye looked sideways at nothing, a dead, milky reminder of some secret he was unwilling to share. "Trust no smile," he hissed instead. "No sweet glance, no turn of the wrist, no scent on a spring breeze."

"I won't," Barro said, tucking the cloak into his saddle bag.

"You truly are a stupid young man. You should turn and ride away as fast as you can."

"Wisdom is for the old, and I have not yet grown a gray hair. I'll live my courage while I can and lament it when I'm too decrepit to do anything else." He mounted his horse and offered a smile to the trader. "When all this is over, I hope to see you again where I can tell you how right you were."

"If we cross paths again, you will not be as you are now. I pray you find your wisdom before you reach that door, boy."

Barro chuckled and reined his horse back to the East and onto the kingsroad. "Come see me when I am crowned prince!" He called back as he rode away. "I'll make you a duke for this!"

His horse trotted in a merry gait as they made

their way towards the front gates of the castle. The day was bright and fair, and the realm gleamed like a pearl in the afternoon sun. Whether true danger lay within those white stone walls or not, it would certainly be a tale to tell when all was done.

Barro couldn't keep the smile from his face. No matter how this ended, all was perfect right now.

*****

"So you've come to solve my daughters' riddle, have you? And who are you that you are so clever? Why will you succeed when so many before you have failed?"

Barro looked up at King Weyn, remaining on bended knee unless and until bidden otherwise. The king was overweight with a merry face, long from the years he spent in battle earning his crown. His face was open and kindly, a face Barro knew he could come to like quite soon.

"Because I am a man who has had to be clever his whole life, Your Grace," he said, looking at the twelve women sitting on either side of the king. "How hard could it be to figure out the minds of a few girls?"

King Weyn threw his head back and laughed, the sound booming around them all.

"I like you!" He declared. "You are a stupid boy, but all before you weren't. Perhaps you will prevail after all."

Barro's smile was firm but confident. He would prevail. There was no choice.

Behind the king were six thrones on either side, and in them, his daughters. Not one of them seemed very interested in the newcomer except as a bug to be squished. He was used to such disdain from royalty, though for different reasons. The nobility did not often look kindly upon common rabble entering their space.

In this case, he was directly challenging the women in their own home.

"If you can solve the mystery of where my daughters go every evening," the king went on, "you may choose whichever one you wish to be your bride."

The twelve dark glares sent his way was immediate and piercing, and he found it charming. Which of these fair birds would he choose to be his wife in the end? The beautiful and seductive eldest princess Hairenrod? The sweet and innocent looking youngest, Yaga? Any of the glorious and varied lovelies in between?

"If you fail," King Weyn said. "Your life is forfeit to the crown. Do you accept these terms?"

"I do, Your Majesty," Barro replied promptly. He did not need to think about it. If he did, he might remember the old man's warnings, or the list of names of the men who entered this castle and never came out again. This was a mission of daring, not logic. Pluck, not caution.

"Magnificent! Then we shall prepare a room for you and see to your every comfort during your stay. Every morning I will ask you for your answer on the reason for the state of my daughters' dresses and shoes. If on the third day you fail to give a satisfactory answer, you will be taken immediately to the dungeon to await execution."

Hairenrod cracked a smile, and Barro fought the urge to smile back. She would be a joy to bend to his will.

"I am your humble servant," Barro said, bowing his head.

The king motioned for a servant and then for Barro to stand. "We will have a feast for you tonight to mark the occasion. Rest for now, my friend. Your work will begin soon enough.

Rest did not come easy, but he managed to drift in and out of a restless sleep. Barro only knew the passage of time from the movement of the sun as it drifted along the large open window in his room. It was the chamber of a servant, yet it was the finest one he'd ever slept in in his life.

When he was prince, what would his rooms be like then?

The servant assigned to look after him came to fetch him for dinner just as the sun began to dip below the horizon. He wore his nicer tunic and trousers, one of two sets brought for the road, and followed the man down the winding corridors to the dining hall.

It's good to have a guide or else I would be lost here for days trying to find my way.

The king and his daughters were there, and no one else. No courtiers or visiting dignitaries or ambassadors. When he was prince, that would have to change as well. What kind of a merry court did not host others at feasts?

Despite this, the finest of foods was laid out, enough to feed a full court and then some. Meat and bread and fruit were piled onto Barro's plate until it could bear no more, and the meal began in earnest.

"How find you this meal, good soldier?" one of the princesses asked him from across the table. She was Cina, one of the younger daughters, and her gaze was piercing and sharp. He would have to watch out for this one.

"Quite fine," Barro said, struggling to swallow the stringy meat. Was this not a rich kingdom with the finest cooks available? Why would they serve him such a terrible dinner? Did they resent his presence so?

"We have you to thank for it," the lovely Hairenrod said, sipping from her crystal goblet of wine. "You brought it to us."

Barro tilted his head to the side, not understanding her meaning. "Your Highness?"

The twins giggled, the sound a dissonant thrum in his ears where there should be harmony.

"I would have preferred a fatter pony," the youngest, Yaga explained beside him. "But it is better than the donkey last week's traveler brought us."

Barro only just managed to hide his shock, the meat souring in his dry throat. He could not trust himself to swallow without the chance of throwing it back up on the royal table. "You cooked my horse!"

"And why not?" Hairenrod asked, twirling her

fork in another string of the cooked beast. "Are you planning on going anywhere soon? Should you solve the mystery, you shall marry one of us and be crowned Prince of Morvena."

"And should you fail, you shall never leave these castle walls again," Hilde, the second eldest finished. "So you have no need of a horse, do you?"

"Trust no smile," the old man had said. "No sweet glance, no turn of the wrist, no scent on a spring breeze."

He didn't.

And so he merely smiled at Hairenrod and took another bite, forcing himself to swallow. His ever-faithful horse took him to this horrible place. She would have to take him just a little bit further.

*****

That evening, the king allowed Barro to stand watch outside the princesses' chambers. He was given a lantern, a large chair, and a blanket should he get cold. Try as he might, Barro found no comfort in the chair provided. How the previous men all slept through their challenges, he had no idea, for he could barely sit in one spot for a minute before having to adjust again. It was hard and lumpy with what felt like rocks instead of cotton stuffing it.

When he was crowned prince and heir, there would be a great many changes to this place.

"Soldier."

Barro paused his fidgeting and looked over at the princesses' chambers. Yaga, the youngest of the

174

twelve, approached him with a pitcher and goblet in hand. She was easily the fairest of all the sisters with golden hair that fell in gentle curls to her waist and large eyes, one the color of a bluebird, the other the branch it nested upon.

Yaga smiled at him, and it was as if Titania, the Queen of Faerie herself, was in his presence.

He dared not trust it.

"Your Highness," he greeted, dipping his head in respect.

"I thought you might enjoy some wine during the night ahead," she said, indicating her offerings.

Barro accepted both though he eyed the dark red liquid critically. "That's very kind of you, Highness."

"We hold no ill will against you," she said sweetly. "And there is no reason to mistreat you before you have even been given a chance."

He poured himself a full cup and toasted her with it. "I thank you all then. May this be a merry contest of wits."

Yaga giggled and turned to leave. "Oh, it is no contest, good soldier. You will fail as all before you have. We simply see no reason to harm you before then. Assuming you behave yourself, that is."

Then she was gone, back into the room of women and secrets.

Barro might not have been a wise man as the traveling peddler knew, but he still knew better than to drink a drop of anything offered to him unless forced.

Was this the secret behind the other men's

failure?

She said she meant me no harm… I have no choice but to believe her.

He had to assume that he was not the first man delivered wine, nor that it was innocently done. He also knew that staying awake and alert would only prevent the princesses from acting out on their plans. Therefore, Barro shifted one last time and found a position in the mahogany and velvet chair good enough to fake sleep.

Please let me be right…

An hour went by. Then two. Not a sound from the princesses' chambers. He nearly fell asleep for real more than once, but the threat of what would happen if he failed was enough to keep him awake.

Then finally on the stroke of midnight…

"Is he asleep?" Which one was that?

At last!

"Of course he is." Sweet Yaga. "I drugged that wine myself. He'll sleep well until dawn."

"Good." That one was Hairenrod. "Then let's go."

Barro kept his eyes closed and breath even as the door to the princesses' chambers opened and the women filed out. He could feel the soft breeze as they walked by him, one by one, never the wiser that he was not as stupid as the previous men in his spot.

Then he felt the air shift again and two lilac breaths on each of his cheeks.

"Oh, please can we take him with us?" he heard one of the twins say. Maha? Meka?

"We could have so much fun," purred the other.

"No," Hairenrod said from further away. "We must wait the allotted time."

"But sister, we—"

"I said no. Now come."

They each sighed in disappointment and the scent of lilac faded away into the darkness. Barro was left alone.

The moment he knew none of the women remained, he cracked one eye opened. Then the other. He threw the cloak on before any roving guard could come across him or any wanton princess return for her prey. Barro could only hope the old traveler's magic was true and none would sense his presence for as long as he wore the piece.

It didn't take long for him to catch up to the line of princesses. They moved like one long phantom, snaking through the castle's many passageways until they reached an enormous mural. The thing was a true horror to behold.

The painting depicted a battle scene which at first seemed ordinary enough and something every king might have in his keep. Yet as Barro and the princesses got closer, he could make out details brought to light by the few torches alight in the corridor. Ancient armies of Morvena tore through the countryside, pillaging everything in its path. Also depicted were the pagans, destroyed to make way for the modern and civilized world of Barro's time. Closer and closer he looked, at the men ripping babies from their mothers only to smash them against trees and stones, at the beasts of the forest raping maidens while they bled and screamed for mercy, and at the pagan boys burned alive at stakes built at their own homes.

Did he truly want to be prince of a place that displayed a mural like this? Did he want to marry a woman that looked at this horror with all the boredom of a night at court?

Hairenrod reached her hand behind the painting and manipulated something to create a large clicking sound. There was a shudder throughout the corridor, and then the mural pushed inward and to the side to reveal a secret tunnel.

The first part of the mystery was revealed!

"Come," the eldest whispered to the others. "Hilde, close the door after us."

The second eldest stayed behind as ordered while the others each grabbed a lit torch in the passageway. The moment each woman touched it, the flames sparked and sputtered and bloomed into a green fire, illuminating their faces in an evil glow.

Then they descended into the tunnel, Barro close behind.

Deeper and deeper they went, down into a dark tunnel of downward stairs and green torches. It went on so long that Barro imagined there was no end to it and that was the reason for the worn shoes and tired women come every morning.

When at last he thought they could go no further or else find themselves in Hell itself, the secret tunnel came to an end. It opened up into a wide chamber already lit with those same green flames in the women's hands.

The group formed a circle in the middle of the chamber, Barro standing just a few feet away from Yaga.

"Our hearts are bladed, our souls serrated," the women whispered together. The words rubbed together like the dry scales of a snake, and echoed throughout the chamber.

What is this...?

"Our hearts are bladed, our souls serrated." They repeated these words again and again, louder each time until they were nearly shouting it. Each time they did so, it sent a thrill of fear up his spine and goosebumps up his arms and legs.

When he could take it no more, the chanting finally stopped. The eldest daughter turned her head toward a section of the chamber that had no light at all and smiled. "Enter."

Twelve men shambled in from the black, eyes wide and gleaming as though in a waking dream. Some had mindless smiles, other were slack-jawed and expressionless. None appeared to be in command of their own bodies or minds.

They all appeared to be nobodies. Vagabonds, travelers, foreigners who would be missed by no one and despised by everyone, much like the old man who offered Barro a way out of this madness. No doubt their anonymity was the point.

As one, the men separated from one another and stepped into each of the hovels. The princesses followed immediately after, taking one man each for themselves.

What madness is this? Barro thought, inching as

close as he dared. Do they mean to seduce these men?

"Our hearts are bladed, our souls serrated," he heard again in chorus from each of the hovels.

His curiosity would not let him remain cautious any longer. He had to see what was happening with those strange women and their enchanted men. With as busy as they all were, surely they wouldn't notice a silent ghost among them.

Trusting in the magic of the cloak, Barro approached the youngest princess's domain. He heard her before he saw her, humming a soft tune that sounded at once familiar and alien to his ears. A lullaby as dark as the crypt around them filled his ears, nearly drawing him in to join the mysterious man, but he remembered the old man's warnings and refused to give in.

Yaga nearly touched Barro as she walked past him and toward her hapless victim. In both hands she held a thin wire, not unlike that of a harpsichord. He wondered at the meaning of it though he knew he would not like the answer, whatever it was.

The prisoner lay on a cot in her section of the foul chamber, as dumb and uninterested in what was happening as any noble invited to a court obligation.

He only showed some sign of life when Yaga got closer, though it was not enough to save him. His weak mumblings and shifting about only seemed to pique her interest, for the princess focused on him like a lioness locking in on its prey.

She reached down to the hem of her skirt where Barro both feared and anticipated something obscene. Instead, she slid out a thin wire from the hem itself, revealing nothing else but an ankle and shapely calf.

"You're in luck, my sweet," Yaga murmured to the man on the cot. "I'm in fine spirits tonight."

The man just stared over at her dumbly. Barro doubted he understood a single word she said to him.

"Do you know why?" She asked. The youngest seemed not to care that she was having a one-sided conversation. She twirled the wire around her fingers and held it tight as she stepped closer. When her bosom was pressed up against the man's side, she leaned over and smiled that same sweet smile she offered Barro only hours before.

Just like Barro, the man appeared dazzled by such a smile from such a creature.

"Because you found me on such a delicious day. There is a man in the castle tonight, and how I wish you were he." Yaga slid the wire up the length of the man's shirt until it neared his collarbone. Then she allowed it to trail back down the center of his chest, partially dragging the rough fabric with it as it went.

Her poor victim simply lay there, unknowing and uncaring to the beautiful girl's actions.

Then she looped the wire around her prey's arm and pulled tight.

Only when the first limb came off did the man finally react.

181

The pupils of his eyes contracted so much that they disappeared altogether and all Barro could see was the green and whites of his eyes. His entire body seized and flailed, and though he struggled, Yaga's restraints held him securely to the black cot.

"Yes!" The youngest princess cried with joy. "That's what I want from you."

She leaned forward again, her hungry wire bloody and hungry for more.

If he had to watch any more of this, Barro was sure he would vomit and give himself away. So he did what any sane man would do in this position.

He ran.

Each hovel Barro passed was filled with similar horrors as the one he left behind. One sister worked on a man with knives, flaying him alive with glee. Another was securing a contraption over her man's head that held rapidly rising water meant to drown him.

Each and every princess had her own victim to torture and murder according her own whims.

As long as the trip down took, Barro's flight back up the stairs seemed to take only minutes. Barro looked over his shoulder constantly, afraid to see the twelve on his heels at any moment.

*****

It was only through some divine guidance that Barro found his way to the king's chambers. The labyrinthian nature of the castle was made worse at night, and the king's tower was well-encased in the center. But at last he reached the hall of portraits where all past kings were hung in proud display, guarding their son in his noble pursuit. Just that morning, Barro would have shivered at the mere thought of his portrait joining theirs one day.

To Hell with all of that now. He had a kingdom to save.

When he reached the center at last, he pushed through the kingsguards with a final grunt of effort and entered King Weyn's private chambers.

"Your Majesty!" He cried, not caring if he woke the whole of the palace now. "Your Majesty, please wake up!"

When he found the king, however, he was not asleep in bed as he expected. All the candles were lit in the king's chambers, and had been for some time. The chambers themselves were decorated in a pale mockery of the princesses' dungeon, draped in black and green silks.

What is this?

The king himself was seated upright in the center of his bed, the satin sheets wrapped about his naked body like an enormous baby. He rocked back and forth, a macabre metronome, babbling to himself in a tongue indecipherable. Nothing remained of the stately monarch Barro met only hours before. It was as though the man might never had existed at all, for this creature of spittle and giggle could hardly compare to the man he once was.

"What have they done to you?" Barro breathed, fixed to the spot as he took in the obscenity before him. Was it not enough what he'd seen within the bowels of the castle, but that the princesses' foul influence had somehow made its way to the king's chambers as well?

"Welcome, young man, welcome!" King Weyn cried, leaning back to look at Barro. He held onto his ankles and grinned, an unhealthy shine in his bulbous eyes. "Have you come to solve the riddle?"

Barro stepped closer, looking around him in case one of the witches had stayed behind with her father. "I have solved it," he said. "And I swear I will free you of this sorcery."

The sovereign threw his head back further and laughed so sharply that Barro jumped in surprise. "That's what the others all said!" King Weyn said. "And then they are the ones set free. Free, my boy!"

"The others? Your Majesty, how long have you been like this?"

But the king simply resumed his rocking, giggling to himself like one of his monstrous daughters. Barro would get no more use from him like this. It was a pitiable sight, and worse, it was a mockery of Barro's own promised suffering if he did not escape this place.

"I will free you," he said again, wrapping the cloak tight around him like the protective shield it was. And as he faded from the king's view, he imagined the horrors occurring beneath their feet, deep in the haunted bowels of the palace.

These witches would be stopped, and he would be the one to do it.

He just didn't know how.

The next morning, Barro forced himself to act as though nothing strange at all had passed. He'd made it back to the uncomfortable chair with just enough time to feign sleep again before Hairenrod and her sisters returned to their chambers to sleep the rest of the night. They whispered and giggled amongst themselves, about what unholy thing he could only imagine, and he could feel their eyes upon him as they passed.

Did they know? Did they suspect at all? Or was their sorcery masked by the power of the old traveler's cloak?

Barro did not know and nor did he wish to. If they knew anything at all, they hid it cleverly behind soft smiles and flirtatious glances. Their initial ire against him from the day before disappeared, and they now welcomed the challenge of his presence with coos and compliments.

As promised, he trusted none of it.

"I do hope you did not sleep the entire night, good soldier," the princess Mim simpered, curling an arm through his. "Father would not be pleased, and we do so enjoy your company."

Just last night I saw you flaying a man alive, Princess, he thought, forcing a smile upon his face. I want none of your enjoyment.

King Weyn was already seated and waiting for them when they all arrived at the table, his eyes clear and his demeanor seemingly untroubled. "Welcome, my daughters. Welcome, young Barro."

Barro nearly forgot to bow, but Mim tugged him down as she curtsied in greeting to her royal father.

"I have been told by the servants that your dresses and shoes are all ruined," the king said after all were seated. "The mystery goes on, it seems."

Hairenrod and the others only snickered and went about the breaking of their fast. Barro reached for a thick roll and a ham steak, knowing he must appear as though nothing were wrong though he wanted nothing more than to strike down the demons around him.

I am only an ignorant challenger, he reminded himself. I know nothing.

He felt the king's heavy gaze and turned to him, a dumb smile on his face. "Your Majesty?"

"Have you discovered anything during your first night, soldier?" King Weyn asked. "You have not forgotten that you owe me an answer each morning, have you?"

Barro looked at the king for a long moment, searching his face for the same insanity that had taken the poor man only hours before. Yet there was nothing to even hint of the sorcery the women had over him. He was as merry and unknowing as the day Barro met him.

True witchcraft indeed.

"I…" Barro looked at the princesses around the table and noticed how they watched him. Their eyes all glittered wickedly, and his courage failed him. There was still more to learn and if the king did not believe him, there was too much danger in revealing what he knew.

"No, Your Grace," he said instead. "I have not forgotten, but I am afraid I drifted off during the night. I have no answer for you this morning."

The women all smiled and he breathed a sigh of relief.

The meal went down a little easier.

Barro kept to himself for most of the day, not wanting to interact with servant nor royal. He was allowed access to the king's library where books of demonology, torture, and every other kind of evil deed and magic might be found amongst the tomes of history and law. Whether the librarian himself was in league with the princesses or under their spell was uncertain, but it was a risk Barro had to take.

"How is it that a man like you is even literate?" The librarian commented while he was pouring through a book of alchemical methods from a neighboring kingdom. The late queen was from another nation, perhaps she had something to do with it?

"I didn't think soldiers were taught to read."

"I had a life before I was a soldier," Barro grumbled, wishing the man would leave him in peace.

"And what life was that?"

Both men jumped at the new voice so close. Princess Yaga appeared as though by magic, just as lovely as Barro remembered her from the previous night. She wore a yellow gown that brought out the gold in her hair and the unusual mismatch of her eyes.

Oh, she would make such a lovely wife, murderous witch though she was...

"Your Highness! I did not see you there." The librarian lowered himself into a deep bow. His reaction broke Barro from his frozen state. He shoved several of the books he was reading beneath one about the history of Morvena and got to his feet to bow as well.

"Good afternoon, Princess Yaga," he greeted.

"You remember which one I am," she blinked. "I'm impressed."

He looked up and couldn't help but smile a little. She truly did look pleased at being called by her name. "You are quite distinctive, Your Highness. I could not mistake you for any of your sisters, fair though they are."

Yaga shrugged and looked away. "It is hard to stand out when one has eleven elder sisters."

"I only have one elder brother," he said. "But I do have some idea of what you mean."

She nodded and approached, head tilted in curiosity. "What is it you are reading, good soldier?"

Barro swallowed thickly and remembered his courage rather than the look in her eyes as she sliced off an innocent man's arm. "The history of Morvena, Your Highness."

"Interesting."

He shook his head and forced a smile. "It truly isn't, as I'm sure you know. But it helps to pass the time until my true work begins."

She laughed then, and he imagined it was a real one. "Well said," she said. "Though I might suggest a better way to pass the time. Would you care to

188

take a turn with me through the castle grounds? My sisters have all gone off on their own and I find myself wanting for company."

"I would enjoy nothing more, Your Highness."

The pair walked arm in arm out of the library and away from any answers Barro hoped to find there. Clever.

His only chance now was to get information from the murderous creature herself and avoid the allure of her presence at the same time.

They did not speak again until they reached the main gardens. They were originally designed by the queen not long after her coronation and kept up in her memory. And whether she was the origin of the evil in this castle or not, Barro had to admit its great beauty.

"I've never seen the likes of this place," he admitted when they stepped out onto the grounds. They passed no less than a hundred varieties of flowers and trees, each cultivated to perfection. Barro could smell the fragrance of the blooms as they walked by, each more tantalizing than the last.

"It was her pride and joy," Yaga said. "Perhaps more so than we."

"I don't believe that's true, Your Highness," he said. A little flattery wouldn't hurt his chances at getting close to her.

Besides, he thought, I'm not lying.

Yaga shrugged and reached up to run her long fingers along the blossoms of a cherry tree. "Perhaps," she said. "But she did love her gardens. So much so that she brought each of us into it."

When he looked at her in askance, she smiled softly, and he could almost believe he was simply on a walk with a pretty girl.

"On the days we were born, Mother ordered a different tree to be planted for each of us." Yaga tilted her head leaned up to breathe in the cherry's sickly-sweet perfume. "This one is mine." Then she paused and flicked her mismatched eyes back at her companion. "You never did answer my question."

"And what question was that, Your Highness?"

"What was your life before you became a soldier?"

Barro took the knife from his belt and cut a cherry blossom with one flick of his wrist. He offered it to her, hating how he enjoyed the curve of her lips as she took it in her pale fingers. "Why do you wish to know?"

"Well," Yaga twirled the bloom in her fingers and held it to her nose to smell, and he noticed the calluses on her hands where years of holding her wire had worn the delicate flesh. "If you are to join my family in one way or another, shouldn't I know more about you?"

From any other maiden, this would be music to his ears. Even knowing who and what she was, Barro felt a guilty thrill rush through him.

"I studied at the monastery near my village," he said even as he knew he should give her nothing. The most innocent piece of information could give her power over him for all he knew.

"The monastery?" She asked. "Why?"

"I am the second son. My elder brother was set

190

to inherit the family business, therefore all that was left for me was to join the priesthood as was tradition."

Yaga nodded and looked up from her flower. "And how did you become a soldier then? It does not seem a likely profession for a peaceful monk."

Barro took the cherry blossom from her and gently slipped it behind her right ear, careful not to touch her skin. "I am a man who craves adventure," he admitted. "A quiet monk's life is not for me, I'm afraid. I make a better soldier."

"And perhaps a better prince?"

He chuckled. "Perhaps."

The youngest princess laughed as well and reached to slip her arm through his once more. As she did so, her hand brushed against the small leather pouch attached to his belt that held his beloved cloak and knocked it loose.

It took only a moment for an ornate golden ring to accidentally catch the ragged fabric, and it was pulled free of its safe container.

Barro reacted immediately.

"No!" Barro's hand jerked out to catch the cloak before it even touched the ground.

The princess flinched back, her eyes wide with alarm.

"I apologize, Your Highness," Barro said with a nervous laugh. "It's just that this cloak is so old and ragged and I do not wish to get your fine dress dirty." He tucked the material beneath the arm furthest from her, his heart pounding with fear. If she had accidentally discovered what it was, if she even suspected…

"I see." Yaga nodded, but her lips pursed, and she kept her hands folded in front for the rest of the walk.

In fact, all of her remained inward for the rest of their time together. They spoke no more of families or destinies, and instead kept the topics to the garden itself and Barro's time in the army. Whatever he might have been able to glean from Yaga was hopeless now. And when he escorted her back to her room, all he received was a cold goodbye and a shut door for his efforts.

I truly have no luck with women, he sighed. Not even among the deviant witches of the world.

*****

That night, Barro did not have to wait nearly as long for Yaga to bring him the drugged wine, nor for the princesses to emerge once he feigned sleep. Now that he'd proven himself not a threat to their secret, Barro supposed they were eager to forget him in favor of their grisly pastime.

After all, they believed he would fail and soon be theirs regardless.

Again they filed one by one to the macabre tapestry of the taking of Morvena, and again Barro stayed close behind beneath his enhanced cloak. He stayed near the sweet Princess Yaga, not only because he knew her movements better than the others' which made her safer, but more importantly, to catch the lingering scent of cherry in the stale dungeon depths.

"Hurry," Hairenrod reminded her sisters. "We must be back before the fool wakes."

"He is no fool, sister," Yaga said, her blue eye glowing beneath the light of the green torch in her hand.

All paused on the stairs to look at her, including Barro.

"What did you say?" the eldest asked in disbelief.

"He isn't," Yaga insisted. "He's actually quite intelligent, and—"

"Yaga spent the whole day with him. I saw them together," said one of the sisters. Gana, Barro thought her name was.

"Is this true?" Hairenrod asked Yaga.

The youngest blushed but did not deny it.

"We don't have time for this," Hilde hissed. "If Yaga wants to play with the man before the end, let her. It changes nothing."

Yaga and Gana glared at each other, but the discussion was over. The descent into the torture dungeon continued in an uneasy silence as Barro wondered what poor souls would suffer this evening for the women's foul tempers.

When they reached the chambers below, he was surprised to find no evidence of the carnage from the night before. No blood upon the stones, no discarded clothing or boots, not even the scent of death lingering in the air. Nothing but the fragrance of flowers and a dark warning in the air.

The women formed their circle as they had

before, the green torches flickering and dancing with evil promise. One by one, the princesses stepped by him to form a circle as they had the night before, already whispering the words he knew would haunt him for years to come.

"Our hearts are bladed, our souls serrated…"

One of the twelve was slower to join her sisters, and he did not realize it until it was too late.

There was a rush of air and the feel of his cloak sliding off to the ground. Barro froze, his heart seizing in his chest so tightly that he lost the ability to breathe.

No… please no…

"You were too obvious," Yaga whispered, for his ears alone. "Protecting that old thing like a holy shroud. And you stood far too close to me to not notice your presence."

"A spy!" exclaimed Inna, the middle sister.

"A spy," hissed the twins, Maha and Meka.

Yaga looked to the eldest sister for guidance, as did all the others. "Hairenrod, what do we do with him? None of the men have ever—"

"You thought you were so clever, didn't you?" Hairenrod purred, approaching Barro with all the tranquility of a serpent and twice the danger. "You thought you could win the challenge."

"I have won," Barro said, sounding more confident than he felt. He lifted his chin in defiance as he stared down the leader of the savage princesses. "I discovered your secret and that means this wicked sorcery ends, Your Highness. One of you will be my bride and I will become heir to this kingdom."

She laughed, her sisters echoing after. It was like the tittering of sirens just as a sailor realized his fate, and Barro wondered what new horror was about to be sprung.

"You will become the heir to grave dust. To swamp slime and to the creatures beneath it. That is the only kingdom waiting for you, Barro of nowhere."

Barro lunged forward but the sisters were upon him in an instant. He struggled against the women holding him fast, glaring at the leader of the princesses with hatred. "I will destroy you, witch."

Hairenrod laughed, and this time she sounded nothing like the alluring creatures of the sea. No, this was the laugh of a serpent hidden and waiting to strike. This was an ugly laugh. "You can try, soldier."

She nodded to her sisters and he found himself dragged toward her conclave. She would not break him, he decided. No matter what she did, no matter how badly she treated him, he would remain strong. Even if he perished and the stones themselves were the only witnesses to his brave end, he would not falter.

The bindings on the cot were tighter than he expected, for all the victims he'd seen were sedate and willing while he was anything but.

"So you've come to stop us, have you?" Her voice. Again, her voice. How could he have ever considered her for a bride, even for an instant?

"I've stopped worse than you," he spat, refusing

to listen to the fear in his heart. He would survive this, he had to!

"Come then, soldier. Come and see if you have what it takes to stop us." Hairenrod smirked in the face of his bravery, as though he were nothing more than a child acting the part of a knight.

"You don't know what I'm capable of."

She reached for a thick strip of cotton and dipped it into a nearby basin of water, making sure to soak it thoroughly. "Perhaps not," she admitted. "But I know my sister, and what she's capable of. I know you cannot bend her to your will. Did you think she would make an ally for you? Is that what you were after?"

Yaga was cruel and merciless. She'd unveiled him and left him to the mercy of her cruel and merciless elder sister. Only a true fool would believe she could be turned from her dark path and make a worthy ally.

And yet even now…

Hairenrod looked into his eyes and scowled as she found him wanting.

The cloth went over his face, blocking all air from entering his lungs.

Barro gasped and sucked in water and cloth in a desperate attempt to breathe. He struggled harder against the restraints that held him. Once when he was a younger man, he'd been taken prisoner by the neighboring kingdom's forces.

The fear he felt then was nothing compared to what he felt now under the wicked Hairenrod's power.

Then the cloth was removed and the dank air of
the torture chambers tasted as sweet as a Spring
garden as Barro filled his lungs. He gasped and
strained, his heart beating so hard in his chest that it
was painful. Such a simple, effortless thing she'd
done, yet it nearly undid him.

She did not wait for him to recover before the
wet cloth was put back on his face and the torment
begun again.

Too many times they went through this dance of
stolen breath, and with each one, Barro was given
less and less time to recover. His lungs burned, his
heart fluttered weakly like a dying bird, and all the
while, the screams of the dying men and the
laughter of women in other conclaves like his made
for less than comforting company.

The last thing he saw as he lost consciousness
was Hairenrod's striking green eyes staring down at
him, delighting in his torment.

Barro could only hope he would be dead before
this went on much longer. Even a brave soldier had
his limits, and Hairenrod so easily found his.

*****

He woke the next morning just before dawn in that
same damned chair by the princesses' chambers,
and if it weren't for the air still burning in his lungs,
Barro might have thought it some nightmare
brought on by the drugged wine.

"Good morning, my dear boy!"

Barro looked up blearily and met the glazed

eyes of King Weyn. The monarch was thankfully clothed this time, but the dangling rapier at his side did not make the soldier feel any better about the situation. "Your Majesty?"

"I came to see how you were getting on. Have my girls set you free? Do you fly? Have you seen the green, my boy?"

Seen the green…?

Barro nodded, unsure of who or what he was even talking to in the form of the king. "I have seen the green flames," he said. "And I have solved the riddle. I wish I could tell you so you would understand."

The light of the dawn crept in through the open windows of the corridor. The lighter their surroundings became, the clearer King Weyn's eyes were. He blinked once, twice, and then shook his head as though to banish some dark dream.

"Riddle?" He asked. "Have you now?"

Barro nodded again, hoping this time that the king was truly returned from the nightly spell the women had him under. "I have," he said. "I know what the princesses do every evening that ruin their clothing and shoes and leave them exhausted."

"And what is that?" The king frowned and narrowed his eyes.

The door beside them opened and the twelve emerged one by one.

The soldier continued on. This was his only hope if he was going to survive both the king's penalty and the princesses' evil whims.

"They take nameless prisoners to the bowels of

the castle and torture them," Barro said, meeting Hairenrod's eyes. He expected to see fear or even anger in her, but there was neither. No, she appeared almost triumphant at his declaration. Was she mad as well? Was the whole of the realm insane?

"How dare you," the king hissed, his hand resting on the rapier's handguard. "You dare to accuse Their Highnesses of such things when you have not risen from this chair either night you stood watch? Do you think me stupid, boy?"

"I think you bewitched!" Barro cried. He held his hands out in front of him as if in prayer. "Sire, I know what they've done to you. I know what they're capable of."

"You know nothing. Now not another word on the matter or I will have you thrown into my dungeon and forget you were ever there."

Barro opened his mouth to argue, but the look on the king's face convinced him otherwise. If he attacked the man's daughters again, it would not be the women he need fear but the royal executioner.

Can I really blame him? Would I believe me were I in his place?

He looked at Yaga whose face was lacking all expression. Even her mismatched eyes showed no hint of satisfaction in the state he was in. Could it be he was slowly earning an ally after all? Was there still hope?

"I apologize, Your Majesty," he murmured, lowering his eyes back down to the ground. "I just… I've had a nightmare, that is all. I did not mean what I said."

The king nodded, though his eyes still burned with anger. "Forgiven this one time," he said. "Now, do you have any useful information for me? Or shall I spend the rest of my days surrounded by misbehaving daughters and useless men?"

He wanted to. Oh, how desperately he wanted to say it again, but he couldn't.

"No, Your Majesty. I need one more night."

"One more," King Weyn said. "After that, your fate belongs to me."

The moment the king left, Barro ran.

They were never quite far behind, taunting and laughing wherever he went. No matter what corridor or door he tried, there was always one of the twelve behind it, thwarting any chance of escape. Even Yaga played along, and if she were on his side at all, it was hidden beneath a thick layer of malice.

There were so many of them that there was no hope of escape, no way of out-maneuvering them. Not in the odds of twelve against one.

For the first time since this venture began, Barro realized there was no getting out of his fate. Even under Hairenrod's cruel hand, he had the hope of escape through death.

Finally, Barro found a room he could retreat to, and there he stayed for the remainder of the day. He did not emerge for food nor for any other reason for the remainder of the day. While the sun was in the sky, he was still partially protected.

At least, he hoped so.

The princesses, however, had other plans.

"You cannot escape us," the twins sang through the door.

"Open up and face us like a man," Hairenrod ordered.

Barro looked from side to side, his eyes darting to every corner of the room in search of a proper weapon. "Witches deserve to burn," he spat. "Not die in honorable battle like a man."

There was nothing.

"He's no man," Hilde laughed. "He's a coward too afraid of a few women to open the door."

The others laughed again and the taunting renewed in earnest.

Barro had no other recourse but to listen to it and watch the sun's journey across the sky. And as he watched, he realized he'd never seen the sky so blue before, so very lovely. Was it always this color? Had it always resembled Princess Yaga's one blue eye?

The hours went on, both painfully slow and yet too fast for a man potentially facing the last hours of his life. There were regrets, many of them, not the least of which involved a ragged cloak left in the dust downstairs. Yet as sunset approached, and the magnificent blue shifted to an array of rubies and citrines, Barro found peace despite it all.

The sun set, and he knew it was time to face what waited beyond, be it the doors or the curtains of life.

He took a breath. Let it out. Savored it as a man does on his way to the gallows.

Then Barro opened the door and faced the twelve.

His third journey down to the dungeons, surrounded on all sides by the twelve, was faster than any time before though his feet dragged and his steps stumbled. Every time he tried to catch Yaga's eye, he found her looking the other way or in whispered conversation with one of her sisters. And as he only had promises of violence from the others, Barro found his walk a quiet and somber thing.

I will kill them for this, he thought to himself over and over. I will find a way out of this yet and each vile creature will die.

So long as Yaga did not resist… so long as she did not fight back, she might yet be spared.

"Our hearts are bladed, our souls serrated."

At first he thought he imagined the whispers, they were so quiet. Then they emerged into the chambers below and the whispers turned into low murmurs.

"Our hearts are bladed, our souls serrated."

The green torches flared and sputtered at the words, and he knew the castle was theirs once more.

"Our hearts are bladed, our souls serrated!"

The words grew louder and louder under they were being shouted, louder than any time in the two previous nights.

Barro was thrown in the center of their circle like a bait animal waiting for its attacker. The air was charged with giddy excitement, as if the girls were preparing for a grand party instead.

Perhaps this was simply their version of it.

"Who shall have him, sister?" Nona asked Hairenrod.

"Please let it be us!" The twins said, green torches lighting four eager green eyes.

Hairenrod smiled and immediately looked to Yaga. "Take care of him for us," she said. "Finish what I started last night."

The youngest nodded and Barro was ushered to her hovel this time amidst the complaints of the other sisters, now stuck with mere peasants to play with instead of the man who plagued them so.

The moment Barro was tied down to her cot, Barro was left alone with the youngest princess, the first time since their meeting in the gardens.

"Don't do this, Yaga," he said when she approached. "Set me free. Help me stop them."

"You still believe I would betray my sisters for you?" She asked, an eyebrow rising. Her blue and brown eyes both narrowed at him.

In the distance, the screams of the other men began in earnest. The women were in a lusty mood that night.

"I believe you know this is wrong. I believe you care for me."

"Perhaps you should not rely so much on your beliefs and instead trust what your eyes and ears tell you." Was it his imagination or did she seem unsure of her own words?

"Then trust in your own eyes and ears. I would have chosen you to be my bride," Barro said.

"It makes no difference," Yaga said, her eyes

flicking over to her victim for a moment before fetching her wire from the hem of her dress.

"What if it did make a difference?" he asked. "What if we could stop this, Yaga?"

The princess twirled the wire around her fingers and contemplated it with sad, mismatched eyes.

"Yaga. Yaga, look at me."

She looked at him.

He smiled at her. "Set me free, princess. Be my queen. Be more than what Hairenrod tells you to be."

Then his princess smiled back at him and he felt hope for the first time in days.

Yaga looped the wire around the base of a toe.

Paused.

Pulled.

*****

He was the last man to ever willingly step foot inside King Weyn's castle in the hopes of learning the princesses' elusive secret. What happened to Barro himself, no one ever really knew. He disappeared like so many before him and was soon forgotten by all who knew him.

All but one.

The following spring when traders came back, one tent in particular was erected just on the outskirts of the village marketplace. The old man running it largely kept to himself, he and his daughter who he was careful to protect against villagers looking for easy prey.

Therefore, on that one summer's day when he

heard an unusual sound not far from his tent, he was swift to assume the worst. He ushered his daughter inside and peeked out to investigate.

He thought it was an animal at first, some sort of wounded creature dragging itself along the ground. It groaned and moaned in its torment, and even if it meant no harm itself, it would soon attract others who did.

Knowing the kinder thing to do was to put the thing down, the man took a long blade and approached.

"Father?" His daughter called from the tent. "What are you doing?"

"Stay where you are, girl," he called back. "I will be back in a moment."

He walked carefully toward the wounded beast, not sure if it would attack or simply cringe away. One could never be sure when it came to something at the end of its life.

When he got closer, a shiver of fear ran up his spine despite the warmth of the day. This was no animal, but a man.

Or, at least, it used to be.

It was a miracle this man was even alive, mutilated as he was. His nose was missing, his lips, his ears... but that was hardly the worst of it. He crawled along the ground, because he had no hands no feet to do it with. Everything beneath the knees and elbows were cleanly severed and seared shut from what appeared to be an iron. The closer the man looked, the more he saw taken. Even the man's personal dignity was not spared his tormentors attack.

A shredded cloak was draped around his otherwise naked body. A cloak he knew very well.

Finally noticing him, the poor creature looked up at him and giggled, pointing up at him with the stump of his left arm. "I've seen the green!" he cried. "Have you seen it? It's beautiful."

The old man lowered his blade and stared for a moment with his one good eye, unsure of what he was even seeing before him. "You are that soldier," he breathed. "The one who saved my daughter."

"Daughters? I love the daughters. I love all of them, all twelve." Barro rolled to his back, and the mirth fled from him as soon as it arrived. "She smelled like cherry blossoms and blood. Oh God, so much blood…"

"I told you to never step inside that castle," the man said with a sigh.

"…eratted…"

The man frowned and stepped closer. "What did you say?"

"Hearts bladed, souls serrated. Hearts bladed, souls serrated." His eyes were glazed, unable to process whatever had been done to him. It was a miracle he'd survived this long as he was.

A miracle or a curse?

"Hearts bladed, souls serrated."

Barro sobbed as he said it over and over, the tears mixed with the dirt and blood on his ruined face.

The traveler knelt beside him and wrapped his old cloak close to the soldier's ruined body. "I'm so sorry," he said. "I should have stopped you. You saved my daughter's life and I repaid you with this fate."

"Hearts bladed, souls serrated."

The man pulled his blade once more, making sure it lined up perfectly. Barro deserved nothing less.

"I'm sorry, young man. I truly am."

"Hearts bladed, sou—"

22524816R00123

Printed in Great Britain
by Amazon